Blackberry Mornings

Happy Birthday!
Jenny
Blessings of joy
on your life
Lisa

Lisa Harris

Cover Art by June Littlepage
Cover Design by Tracy McCoy

Laurel Mountain Press
P.O. Box 2218
Clayton, Georgia 30525
www.laurelbooks.com

Printed in the United States of America

Dedicated:

In memory of my daughter, Whitney Ann (1983-2009)
whose laughter will forever sing in my heart,
her passionate love for children was a gift to many
and her servant nature was truly inspiring.

"Do not be afraid. I have redeemed you.
I have called you by name - you are mine." Isaiah 43:1

A Blackberry Morning

"Why is that kitchen window up," she thought? It was end of July and the August heat was on its heels trickling down her back. Chloe walked over and tugged at the window but it wouldn't budge. "Doggone it," she fussed, using her grandmother's favorite southern expression when she was frustrated with something. Grinning, Chloe also remembered how her family would describe someone that lived in the deep woods of the south. "Why Honey, they are one fine family, although country as cornbread," she would say, "but definitely a fine family." She couldn't help but giggle out loud.

"Hey, what's my beautiful wife giggling about this early in the morning?"

"Oh, just cornbread," she laughed again giving him a hug and kiss.

"Cornbread?" he mused. "Should I ask?" Adam said with one eyebrow cocked looking at her.

"Nah…you Northern boys wouldn't understand."

"You're probably right," he laughed. "Although, I would think that loving a gal from the south makes me half southern."

"In your dreams," she laughed.

"Hey Adam, did you raise this window? I can't get it back down and the cool air is flying out keeping the kitchen hot."

"Oops sorry, I did raise it to kill a wasp and I suppose I forgot."

"No worries, just come shut it for me."

Adam walked over and lowered it in one swoop but not before he caught sight of the blackberry bush outside the window loaded with large, lush berries. He looked over at Chloe and grinned really big. "Ready for a blackberry pie? I'll go right out and pick the bush clean."

Chloe grabbed a wooden bucket and tossed it to him. "Go ahead and I'll sit on the patio with my coffee and watch."

Adam took the bucket and placed it on his head...acting silly as he trudged out the back door with Chloe on his heels. She plopped down in the rocker and he walked over to the bush and preceded to pick.

She sipped on her coffee letting her mind wander. She and Adam had been married for ten years, and for the most part they had all been good ones. Adam was charming, silly, boyishly handsome, very kind and hardworking. There was only one thing that wasn't right, they hadn't been able to have a child. She glanced over at her goofy husband and waved.

At 38, they were reaching the age where it was now or never, but God was silent and she took that as a never.

Tears rolled into her eyes as her heart pondered on never having a child. They had considered alternatives but they were so very expensive and on a worship leader's salary it was too large a debt to consider. Adam strutted over with his bucket brimming with berries, walking like a proud peacock when he realized Chloe's eyes were misty.

He leaned over and kissed her cheek knowing immediately what was in her heart, "It will work out in His time, I promise...we just have to wait." Chloe gave a half smile, while walking her cold coffee to the microwave. But not before she yelled out, "Well tell God I am tired of waiting and I'm getting old!"

Adam stuck his head back in the doorway and said, "remember Sarah was 90 when she conceived!" He ducked just as her flip-flop flew across the kitchen toward his head.

Adam laughed and ran.

Chloe laughed too...he always seemed to lighten her load, and she was grateful.

…

Vickie groaned as she crawled out of bed to see about her one year old crying in his baby bed. At eight months pregnant she had no idea how she was going to take care of both babies. Why oh why wasn't she more careful and why did she think she had to have a man in her life to make her happy? She wished she had met Jesus before Mike had appeared in her life and maybe she would've made different choices. But, what mattered was now and the choices she made today. Vickie picked up A.C.E. and hugged him. She had always loved using initials when saying a child's name, they were the perfect initials for her black haired blue-eyed boy that captured her heart.

"Oh Ace, what's the matter honey?"

"He sniffled and hugged his mommy around the neck."

Vickie warmed a bottle to comfort him and rocked him on her swollen belly.

Her thoughts wandered back to her situation. Abortion had been out of the question. She could not do that, it went against everything in her heart. But, could she do adoption? She had been adopted herself. She wished she had family to help, but her parents were gone and her sister had been placed with another family sealing the records forever. Vickie felt a headache come on just as Ace fell asleep. She awkwardly placed him back in bed and crawled in herself feeling a bit strange.

The next morning, still feeling a bit out of sorts, Vickie got herself ready for work and Ace ready for daycare. She was fortunate that her parents had encouraged her to get her degree as a nurse. She loved working with geriatrics so the town's nursing home became her second home.

First person she saw after dropping off Ace was Ms. Kate, the southern belle of the ward. She swooped around tending to all the others with her gracious and loving demeanor. Ms. Kate was a delight and secretly one of Vickie's favorites.

"How are you this morning Ms. Kate?" Vickie asked.

"Well the question really is how you are with that big belly poking out?" Ms. Kate's eyes twinkled.

Vickie smiled and said, "I'm really fine, just worried how I'm going to do it all by myself Ms. Kate."

"Where's Mike, did he take off again?"

"Yes ma'am, he took off and signed off all his rights for the babies. I made it legal."

Ms. Kate looked disgusted for a moment then changed her tune. "Well, good thing you didn't marry that boy. You can certainly do better for Ace and this one," as she patted Vickie's tummy.

"By the way, Vickie, do you have any family?" asked Ms. Kate.

"The only person I have is a sister, but she was placed with another family when we were adopted. The records were sealed and I've never been able to find her.

Ms. Kate nodded and Vickie walked off to the next patient. Ms. Kate went back to her room and pondered on Vickie's situation. She needed help and while she was still of sound mind, she felt God would give her direction. The first step was calling her grandson Andrew, the attorney. He could help.

Ms. Kate continued to ask Vickie questions about her life and her sister over the next few days, and Vickie was so distracted over her situation she just answered without question. Finally, Ms. Kate had all the information that her grandson needed. He could now try to track down her sister through the legal system.

Daily Ms. Kate would sneak her cell phone out of her apron pocket that she insisted on wearing every day and call her grandson.

"Andrew, do you have any news?" she whispered.

"Well, grandma I just found her sister's address two minutes ago and it's the next town over…what do you want me to do?"

"Let me ponder that a moment and I'll call you back."

Ms. Kate leaned back on her bed as she had been resting. What should I do? She thought. Do I ask Andrew to go over and talk with her sister? Do I tell Vickie or surprise her? Ms. Kate kept pondering and praying for guidance.

Her answer came pretty quickly as she heard the ambulance pull up and found Vickie had passed out and was bleeding profusely. She picked up her cell phone and called Andrew immediately.

"Andrew, please go over and see her sister, explain the situation. It's now imperative that her sister know since Vickie is in the hospital emergency room eight months pregnant."

Andrew hung up and prayed a quick prayer for guidance. He grabbed the address and left.

…

Chloe got off of work and was changing into her running clothes for a quick run before making dinner when the doorbell rang. She quickly pulled on her t-shirt and ran to the door.

She opened to a nice looking man dressed in a dark suit and sporting a brief case.

"Well hello, what can I do for you?"

Andrew smiled and said, "You don't know me, but I am Andrew Taylor, an attorney in Oakland County."

Chloe smiled and said, well come in, my husband should be here soon. Andrew thanked her and sat down.

"I understand that you have a sister." Andrew stated.

Chloe drew back in surprise, "you know I have a sister? Do you know where she is?"

Andrew pulled out some papers verifying their adoptions to two different sets of parents. He spent a few more minutes making sure everything was correct before answering her questions.

Adam walked in through the front door surprised to see a visitor in his family room.

"Hi, I'm Adam, Chloe's husband."

"Andrew Taylor, an attorney in the next town."

"What can we do for you Mr. Taylor?"

"Well, I was just going to answer your wife's questions about her sister."

Chloe turned to Adam and said, "Honey, he's found my sister, Vickie!"

Adam smiled big and said, "Why did you find her sister? Is Vickie looking for her?"

Andrew sat back down and motioned for them to sit for the long story. After telling them about his grandmother's request, and now the sudden urgency to find Chloe since Vickie was in the hospital, he asked, "Do you want to see her?"

"Chloe jumped up, grabbed her purse and said, let's go!" She and Adam drove their jeep following Andrew to the hospital just as the baby was being taken by C-section.

Finally, after a long agonizing hour, the nurse came and got her and Adam, saying, "Things don't look good for Vickie, but her daughter is just fine."

Chloe looked at Adam confused but quickly followed the nurse to her room. Vickie was so very weak from loss of blood she could only whisper.

"Who are you?" she asked.

"Vickie, its Chloe your sister."

Vickie looked up and touched her cheek. "Oh Chloe, I've missed you and needed you so much?" She whispered so softly Chloe could hardly hear.

"Vickie, you'll be fine and I'll help you with the babies. Where's your other child?"

"Oh no" she groaned, "Ace is still at the daycare. Will you go get him so he'll be safe?"

"Of course we will. Can you tell me the number and give us permission to take him?"

Vickie mustered up enough energy to speak to the daycare and made the arrangements. Chloe and Adam left immediately to get their nephew. Chloe felt like she was in a dream. She now had her sister, a nephew and now a niece! God was blessing her with family.

They arrived at the day care and the lady brought Ace out. Chloe was instantly enamored with her nephew and marveled at how much he looked like her sister.

"Ace, I'm going to take you to see your mama." Chloe crooned.

Ace just cuddled right up to her and Chloe's eyes glistened with tears. "Oh Adam, will Vickie be alright? She looked so weak and the doctors are nervous." Adam reached over and grabbed her hand. That was all he needed to do.

They strapped Ace in his car seat the day care provided and took off. It felt like it was a race against time.

But they did make it, Chloe had a couple of hours with her sister before she passed. They held each other, told private things and Vickie asked her to be her babies' mommy before she took her last breath.

Chloe sobbed until Adam took her in his arms. "Honey, we have to take care of Ace right now, and also the baby comes home in two days. We've got to get some things for them…it's what Vickie wanted."

Chloe gathered Ace in her arms and they went to Vickie's home and gathered most of his belongings along with his birth certificate which, as she glanced at it, gasped.

"Adam look at this," she said sticking the certificate under his nose.

He looked up, his eyes filling with tears as he read out loud, "Adam Charles Eaton." It was at that moment she and Adam knew God had given them a sign, Ace was Adams namesake, he was their son.

Two days later, they picked up Lily Rose Eaton, Adam's new baby sister. That morning was bittersweet with the loss of her only sister and the blessing of two babies. Chloe took Lily Rose on the back patio to rock to sleep when she looked over at the blackberry bush. Shocked she motioned for Adam to look.

"Didn't you just pick that bush clean two days ago honey, and now's it's full of huge beautiful berries!"

"Yes, I did." He nodded in amazement as he went over and examined the bush which was amazingly loaded with large juicy blackberries.

"It's God's sign to us Chloe," he said, "To never doubt his timing… for we were barren just two days ago like this bush, and now God multiplied our family from two to four…overnight." Adam said a prayer of thanks, grabbed his wooden bucket and picked God's abundant blessing.

Indeed, it was a Blackberry Morning.

"As water reflects the face, so one's life reflects the heart."
Proverbs 27:19

Just Like
Mama Said...

Grabbing her dish pan of swirling dirty water from all the breakfast dishes being washed, Sadie walked over to the back porch and tossed the water over the railing. She loved washing dishes, it was a mindless chore that she could do while she and God had conversation. Then when the washing was done, she would chuck the water out along with her hurts, disappointments, and all those little sins that kept creeping in on a daily basis. Afterwards, she always felt her spirits lifted up like clouds in the skies.

Outside, since sunrise, Grayson, her husband of five years had already been chopping wood for the stove, getting the hay ready for the cows and all the other demanding chores it took to run their small farm. Sadie was thankful they had a life together, he still made her heart skip a beat with his charming smile and those devilish remarks he'd whisper in her ear as he hugged her at the end of the work day. She would always pretend to be shocked at his boyish behavior but he knew she was secretly delighted.

But enough musing, she needed to head back to the kitchen to plan her day. Sadie whipped out her pencil and paper and begin to write her list. This was something her mama taught her to do...always plan your day, she would say, but be ready for God's detours, for those are the moments that bring the joy. And she was right...as mothers usually are. God always had a detour for her, a person in need, a child in distress, a hungry passerby and today, who knows? Taking a deep breath Sadie got ready for her routine and possible detours.

***

"Oh my word," Caroline muttered to herself, "I cannot believe I did that."

"Did what, Honey?" her husband Max said.

"Oh Max, where did you come from, you shouldn't sneak up behind a woman with a frying pan in her hand," she laughed.

He grabbed her swollen waist and gave her a quick hug. "So what did you do?"

"Oh...I put your stew on the stove to cook and forgot to light it...so, no lunch for you today!" she laughed.

"Hmmm, that could have possibilities," he said with a wink.

"Shoo, get out of here...I'll holler for you later!"

Shaking her throbbing head, Caroline grinned to herself over her husband and his foolishness...could she love him anymore?

Max went on out the door, looking back briefly at his wife. He was a bit worried about her pale skin and tired looking eyes which he supposed was natural when you're entering your ninth month of pregnancy, but still...his thoughts trailed off.

A couple of hours later Max thought he'd better check on Caroline, after he felt a prickling on the back of his neck. He put down his pitch fork and headed toward the house, stopping on the front porch to knock the mud off his shoes.

"Caroline," he called.

Nothing.

"Caroline," he hollered again with no response.

Max looked the small house over, then happened to glance outside the window and saw Caroline on the ground underneath the clothes line.

"Caroline," he yelled as he sprinted to her side, picking up her head he saw that she was barely conscious.

"Max," she whispered..."make sure the doctor saves the baby, don't worry about me."

18

Max hugged her and ignored the comment, too concerned for her at the moment as he picked her up and carried her inside to the bed.

"Caroline, what happened?"

She looked at his handsome rugged face, his green eyes were sharp and probing as he steeled himself to be strong for her.

"I'm not sure, I just became really tired and weak and then I guess, I fainted."

Max got up, and brought her some water making her drink a few sips as he pushed her blonde hair away from her clammy forehead. He took the cup from her hands, and gently covered her with their wedding quilt. He then spoke with firmness in his voice and told her to stay in bed as he was going to get the doctor in town.

Caroline was too weak to protest and sunk further into the pillows, allowing herself to fall asleep…always with her hand on her stomach, praying for protection.

The doctor entered her room and after the examination, he came into the kitchen to speak with Max.

"Max, I'm afraid this isn't good, she is just too weak and fatigued at this stage…something just isn't right. Her glands are swollen, she's feverish and she said she'd been suffering from constant headaches. Has she mentioned these things to you?"

"No, Caroline never wants me to worry, she hides how she really feels." Max felt awful for not seeing her true discomfort, he felt so helpless.

"Well, I'm not sure about this diagnosis, but I think Caroline has what is called leukemia, it's a blood disease that enlarges the organs and causes the same symptoms. I've only seen one other case in the last few years.

"Can you fix this doc?"

The doctor hung his head and said, "I don't think so Max, we just don't know a lot about this aggressive disease."

"You mean she could die?" he asked.

The doctor just stood shaking his head saying, "Max, I don't know how God is going to heal Caroline, but without His intervention, I would say just a couple of months at best."

Max became so nauseous that he sat down, clinching his fists he fought the sick feeling until the Doc put his hand on his shoulders.

"Max, go outside and I'll sit with Caroline...you need to get hold of your emotions before you can be of help to your wife and baby."

"Baby?" Max sputtered. "What about the baby, Doctor?"

"Hopefully, all will be well but first let's take care of Caroline, that helps the baby the most."

Max went outside to clear his head. Just a few hours ago their life was just fine, they were happy together and, happy about the baby coming expanding their family. They dreamed together, laughed and loved together. Max looked up to the heavens with tears streaming down his tormented face and whispered in his heart, why Lord? Why now, why Caroline, why our family? Max fell to his knees crying, praying and, begging for his wife to be healed. No audible answer came...

Days passed and Caroline became so weak she couldn't leave the bed so Max let the farm go as much as he could. He just thanked God their good friends came quickly when they got the word about Caroline. Sadie was Caroline's best friend from childhood, they had shared everything together. Secrets, giggles, dreams and even when Caroline's mother died when she was thirteen, Sadie shared her mother. Later when Caroline married Max, he and Grayson became close friends. Their friendship was a blessing even more so now.

Sadie sat by her dearest friend cherishing those moments. Everything she did for Caroline, every tear she wiped, every meal she cooked and coaxed Caroline to swallow was a privilege. She was humbled by her strength and the grace in which she took the news showing concern only for their baby and Max.

Fall had made its presence known as the leaves swirled in front of the window in Caroline's bedroom where the air was crisp and clear but nobody really noticed. That's because Caroline's contractions had started and were coming fast. Max stayed on one side and Sadie on the other, each holding her up helping her push. The pain gave her much agony but Caroline persevered with each contraction. Grayson had gone to fetch the doctor and after he gave a quick examination, determined the baby would be born after a few more good pushes. He could tell Caroline had completely lost any trace of steam and nodded to Max and Sadie to help her with all their strength. With tearful encouragement to Caroline, the last push gave way to a beautiful baby boy. Max grabbed his wife hugging and crying at the same time. Caroline quietly wept. A few minutes later, she felt an oddly overwhelming urge to push again, and in a frightened state of mind, she felt another baby...but, it just couldn't be. But it was....and this one was a girl, a beautiful little girl.

Overwhelmed, the two parents just stared at the babies. Caroline was too weak to do anything but collapse back on her pillows, so Sadie took over and cleaned and wrapped them both in warm blankets. Max took his son and Sadie laid their baby girl in her mother's arms. Grayson came back in and comforted Sadie as they watched the bitter but oh so sweet moment. After a few minutes they left the parents and went to the kitchen for coffee. The doctor was already sitting at the table, sipping hot coffee as he mulled over what he was going to say. Caroline's vitals were dropping quickly and he didn't think she would last much longer. However, it didn't surprise him when his eyes met Sadie's, he didn't have to say a word...because she knew.

Sadie sank down on the bed next to Grayson and cried. No words, just tears. There wasn't strength enough to do anything else. Grayson wanted her to sleep and Sadie did for a bit, but after that she was up helping her friend with the babies. How could she sleep when her friend was slipping away?

   ***

Sadie crawled in the bed and laid beside Caroline like they did when they were little girls. Sadie stroked her hair telling her how beautiful her babies were. Caroline grabbed her hand saying, "Sadie," she whispered, "will you do this for me?" Sadie's tears trickled down her cheeks, as she shook her head yes remembering their earlier conversation. They would help raise the twins, now proudly named Lily and Landon.

"Remember Sadie, when my mother died? How scared I was? But, you told me not to be scared, that you would share your mother with me, and so you did. What would I have ever done without you and your mom? Now I'm going home and I need you to share your life with my babies...

***

Fall turned into winter and Caroline had been gone for three months now. Lily and Landon were thriving beautifully, but their dad, Max was not doing well. At first, the plan was for Grayson and Sadie to keep the babies temporarily, until he could get things going and figure out his life. But, more and more days started to slip by without seeing him. Grayson tried several times to reach out and help but Max pushed away, angry at God for taking his wife. He felt too numb to bond with the babies which distressed them both.

One day, right before spring made its full arrival, they received a letter from Max. He had moved out to the west to start a new life. He had papers drawn up at the attorney's office for them to sign giving Grayson and Sadie full guardianship over his children. Sadie and Grayson just stared at each other. They never knew how God was going to answer their prayers for a baby. They both loved children, however, after a few years and no pregnancy it was apparent they would not be blessed by any of their own.

So, was this how God was answering their prayers? Through their best friends unbearable loss and continual grief? They knew God could open up Sadie's womb but chose not to, He chose to bless them with their best friend's two babies who needed them. And who was better qualified to talk to them about their parents than themselves. No one.

Caroline in her dying breath, named her children. Lily had been her mother's name and Landon was for the land that she and Max had toiled and made their own. It was also the land her children were born on. They were beautiful names and with a kiss on the top of each head, a blessing of love was bestowed upon them. Caroline passed from earth onto heaven in that moment.

Grayson held tightly onto Lily, he didn't believe he could love her anymore had she been their flesh and blood. Sadie patted Landon's squirming legs and told him about his mother. She knew those words would never end, for they would know their mother as she did. Sadie and Grayson decided to give each child their parent's name, so Lily became Lily Caroline and Landon became Landon Maxwell.

They signed the guardianship papers and sent them back to court. You see, God had His plan all along...and the detour it took was long and very painful, but the blessings born were enormously joyful...just like mama said.

"Delight yourself in the Lord, and He will give you
the desires of your heart."
Psalm 37:4

A Time for Everything

She leaned back with her head resting against her 'comfy chair' as her husband always called it. Sadie purchased it several years ago during a fabulous clearance sale at Macy's. It was over stuffed and married together with several different prints of fabric. Definitely, a country French style that called her name. It was delivered a few days later and gently placed in the Keeping Room next to the kitchen, the heart of their home.

They had their routine, Sadie and Steve, as she woke up at 4 a.m. to start her day with scripture and prayer, then writing in her journal, an intentional keepsake for their child. Steve, on the other hand would rise at 7a.m., push back the covers and hang off the side of the bed for several moments, then slowly make his way to the kitchen to start the second pot of coffee for the morning. By nine o'clock, Sadie was in her office working on her next story and Steve was positioned behind the Pharmacy counter, counting out pills for the sick. A career he loved, and received great satisfaction from.

Their lives were 'normal' if that's a word you can use to describe a family nowadays. Two hardworking people, carving out lives, raising their child and saving for the unknown. They had met later in life, Sadie at 30, and Steve was 35, both marrying for the first time. Their only child came within the first year of marriage, Evie, who was the delight of their hearts. The years clicked on by...every year they became faster, almost as quick as Sadie's hair grayed and Steve's fell out. But, no matter, laughter was the cure, it was the essence of their home.

Evie grew up, and no matter how hard Sadie tried to stop the growing process, she grew without fail. She flourished into a lovely young woman who met and married a man whom they loved and admired. Life was good. Life was golden. Life was changing.

Sadie shuffled around in her 'comfy chair' trying to rid herself of the headache that plagued her. Her favorite pen, a fine point with just the right shade of blue ink fell out of her hand onto the notes she had written. She still believed in the written word, the sweetness of opening up a letter and holding it in your hand to read. It said to the receiver, you were worth the effort and I love you. Steve wrote notes and hid them. Sadie smiled just thinking about all the notes she had found through the years and put them in her 'Sunshine' box. This box contained all her special letters, notes, cards from people she loved. On occasion, Sadie would re-read and her heart would be full with, warm sunshine.

Sadie looked over at the pot of coffee she had made, and forced herself to get up and pour another cup for a possible jolt of energy. That was what she was lacking now was energy and she was only in her mid-fifties. These were the fun years she was told, the years of travel and trying new and different activities, tastes and sounds. Not that she was much of a traveler, no Sadie was a professed homebody, but not Steve, as he was the adventurous type always keeping a constant twinkle in his eyes. That's why his customers loved him, he had such kind eyes.

Looking over the house as she walked with her cup of coffee, Sadie laughed at the mess he had made by his chair. His Bible with notes on the floor, a coffee cup that never made it to the sink and his reading glasses sitting by the phone, as they were the last Americans to still have a landline. Sadie left it, dusting around the cup and glasses, it was familiar, it was home.

Sadie picked up her cell phone to check the time...rarely did you ever see anyone look at their wrist for the time, it was almost like watches were becoming a thing of the past. That was kind of how she felt, a throwback from the past, wondering about the future. Their future, hers and Steve's. Sadie sighed and picked up her Bible and walked back to the bedroom. It was time to read to Steve, yet his eyes said he was no longer there, the twinkle was gone. The horrible illness stole everything from him giving no quality of life. It was a matter of time they said. That's what life's about...time. The Bible says there is a time to weep and a time to laugh, a time to mourn and a time to dance... (Part of Ecclesiastes 3:1-8)

Sitting by his side, Sadie opened to those scriptures and read with a fresh understanding. Gratitude to God was what she chose except for the one regret her heart held onto knowing it would be the last to go. Sadie leaned over Steve and for the hundredth time whispered...I wished I had met you sooner, just so I could have loved you longer.

"Be joyful in hope. Patient in affliction. Faithful in prayer."
Romans 12:12

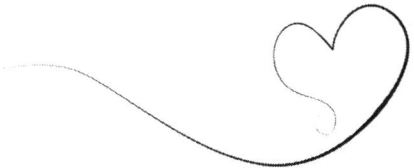

Farmhouse Flip

*H*aving the last box into the back seat of her bright red Volkswagen convertible, Lexi leaned against the car she affectionally christened 'Sweet Red' and pondered over her dilemma. It had been three years since Samuel died, her soul mate for twenty years. They married young, right out of college, in fact, it was the week after graduation. God had been good to them, blessing them with a son they had so longed for, Eli who was now sixteen and driving his dad's truck. Lexi took her hand and pulled her thick reddish blonde hair into a ponytail and off her skin that was beginning to glisten from the morning sun. She had loaded the last box of odds and ends that she needed for the farmhouse.

Even after three years, Lexi still felt the loss of Samuel, but living was getting easier and of course, having Eli brought her joy. Two months ago she was contacted by an attorney in the next county. Lexi agreed to come in and within a few minutes she found herself the owner of her deceased aunt's farmhouse in the next town called, Mapleville. A quaint, almost Mayberry like town dotted with antique stores, sandwich shops and of course, the town barber was front and center on Main Street. Had she not been sitting, her knees might have buckled from the news. What would she do with the farmhouse? Selling it was out of the question, as this home had been in the family for several generations. This farmhouse was part of Eli's legacy, so she would just have to figure out what to do.

Figuring out turned out to be the easy part, it was carrying out the decision that was so hard. With Eli's input, they decided to flip the house, not to sell but to rent until Eli married. After they inspected the farmhouse, feelings of being overwhelmed flooded into her heart. Could she do this? Lexi was the project queen, as she always had several DIY (Do it yourself) projects going and Samuel was always good-hearted to pitch in. He was very talented and could fix anything and make it look fabulous. She had learned so much from him and even Eli seemed to have inherited his father's talent for making rooms come to life. So here they were, anticipating the flip with hopes of bringing the charm back into the home. Lexi just hoped her body would hold out until it was completed.

Grabbing her keys, sunglasses, and ball cap, Lexi pulled her ponytail through the back of her husband's favorite cap and cranked up 'Sweet Red.' She had been so surprised when Samuel had bought this for her 40th birthday, and now five years later, it still purred like it was brand new. She loved to drive with the top down and the wind in her face...it was relaxing and it gave her a sense of being younger, care-free and joyful. Headed to the farmhouse in Mapleville, Lexi passed many beautiful old farm homes, barns, and open pastures. It was a serene drive that she had grown to love.

Memories flooded her heart as she drove through the town. This was the place where she grew up, the farmhouse was the home she so loved to visit and spent many summers playing in the woods pretending she was a princess held captive. Smiling, Lexi remembered the family next door, the Taylors, a great family with several kids that she played with. She wondered what became of that family and if they still owned the farmhouse next to her aunt's property.

Lexi finally got there, unloaded her car and unlocked the side door to the kitchen. Walking in was like coming home. The gigantic fireplace was in the keeping room next to the kitchen...it was so big, she could almost walk into it, truly amazing. Looking around, Lexi noticed that the molding around the doors and windows was still in good shape. The plank flooring was lovely with a beautiful patina that just needed a good cleaning. No problem, she thought. On through the house Lexi walked and made notes. One hour later she made her way back to the kitchen and poured herself a cup of coffee she had brought in the thermos. The warmth coated her throat as she sat in a rocker deciding what projects to tackle first.

Judd Taylor had been outside raking his yard of all the Maple leaves that had accumulated on his property when he saw the little red car slowly ride by his home and turn into the home next door. Curiosity may have killed the cat but it wasn't going to get him because he would just go visit and find out what was going on. He had been to his neighbor's funeral several months ago and wondered what or rather to whom she left her home.

Judd walked back into the farmhouse that he had inherited from his family. His brother and sister took their inheritance in dollars, but Judd wanted the farmhouse to continue the Taylor roots there. However, at 46, he had never married and had settled himself in as a confirmed bachelor. He wanted to marry but just never found the right girl. Judd went into his bathroom to wash up before he went for his 'curiosity visit' next door. Looking in the mirror, he felt like he was a decent looking fella… nothing to swoon at but also nothing to run away from either. Dark brown hair still rather thick for his age, hazel eyes and lightly browned skin from the past summer's sun. He tucked his shirt into his jeans and changed over from work boots to his casual boots and headed out the door.

Deciding to walk the football length distance between the homes, it really took him no time as he had the long legs to cover the distance rather quickly. Peeking in the side door he saw a petite strawberry blonde sitting in the rocker, but couldn't tell what she was doing. Judd tapped on the door with no response. He jiggled the door knob and realized it was open so preceded to walk in…with still no movement from the woman, he reached over and shook her shoulder. Lexi jumped up and screamed in fright and as she did so, tripped over the rocker as she turned to get away. Judd was totally caught off guard with this response and kept trying to tell her he was the neighbor…finally, Lexi calmed down but not before she had her say.

"Oh my goodness, you scared me to death," she said in a loud raspy whisper.

Judd leaned over and held out his hand to help her up saying, "I'm so sorry, I didn't mean to scare you, but when I tapped on the door and you didn't respond, I just walked in."

By this time Judd was looking a bit sheepish and apologetic, and Lexi finally laughed and accepted his apology with a grin. Judd noticed how her eyes lit up when she smiled and liking that feature he tucked that thought in the back of his mind.

Judd held out his hand again, this time to shake hers and introduced himself as Judd Taylor, the neighbor at the next farm over. Lexi grinned again, thinking that name was very familiar and replied her name was Lexi Anderson, the niece to Lily Langley her deceased aunt.

Judd leaned his large frame back onto the wall and stared at the feisty woman before him. Was this the one that made him play the prince that came and rescued her from the treehouse? Judd remembered swords out of sticks and the princess screaming for help as he fought off the enemies…and if he remembered correctly, she had long reddish blonde hair. Judd cleared his throat before he spoke.

"Lexi, are you the one that would come over and play princess in the treehouse?" His eyes were laughing while trying to keep a straight face.

Lexi looked back at him as she remembered his childhood face, "you were my prince, Judd!" then turning bright red, she laughed right along with him. So after an hour or so of reminiscing, Lexi asked him, "Judd what do you do for a living?"

Judd looked around the room and replied, "I'm a contractor and specialize in remodeling old homes like this one."

Lexi's eyes lit up and said, "Could I hire you to help me and Eli remodel this one?"

"Eli," he repeated.

"Yes, my sixteen year old son." Lexi replied.

"So you're married?"

"No, widowed three years now, so it's just me and Eli," Lexi grabbed a broom that had been left in the corner and started to sweep.

Judd pondered that for just a moment before he said softly, "I'm sorry about your husband, Lexi."

Lexi looked up and smiled, "We're fine now…it's just a new normal for us and Samuel left us comfortable so I'm not forced to work while he's still in school. However, in one more year he will be off to college and I think I would like to go back to work. But, for now though, I need to get this farmhouse flipped and rented."

Judd lingered a few more minutes as he wrote down his cell number for Lexi to call when she decided on a contractor. Saying goodbye and walking out the door was a bit hard, and that startled him. It had been quite a while since a woman grabbed his attention like that, and it actually felt good!

Lexi locked the door behind him and felt her knees go a little weak. What a kind man he was, she thought, and not bad on the eyes either. So, they had played together as children, and if she remembered correctly, her Aunt Lily and his mom, Mrs. Taylor had been best friends.

After discussing the situation over with Eli, she made the decision to hire Judd. After all, Eli was back in school for his senior year and would not be available to help with the flip. Judd answered the call with a yes and they made arrangements to meet at the house the next day.

Lexi was, by trade a designer, it was what she went to school for and loved it. She was always helping friends with their décor and the farmhouse would be a special joy that she wanted to savor. What she didn't realize was bringing a contractor and a designer together, both with strong opinions would be quite the challenge.

Judd just stared at Lexi as she described all the physical changes she wanted done. He would jump in and try to tell her that this particular wall was load-bearing. She would just reply, "Okay, figure out how to get around that." Then the bathrooms needed gutting and she wanted pipes moved, and again he tried to explain the cost involved, and once again she would reply, "Okay, figure it out." By the end of the conversation, he was worn out and exasperated and Lexi was perplexed that she had to tell him to figure things out. Wasn't that what he did?

Judd went home that night to 'figure these things out,' as she put it. He already had them 'figured out' what he hadn't been able to do was 'figure her out.' Laughing to himself, he grabbed a towel and headed to the shower…hoping for a way to explain his way of 'figuring.'

Autumn was in full swing as the leaves swirled in the air with the movement of the wind. The cool weather meant cold wood floors in the morning as she crawled out of bed and went to make her first cup of hot brew for the day. Sipping on her coffee, she grabbed her Bible for a few minutes of spiritual feeding and reflection. Lexi missed Samuel the most during this part of her day, as they shared it together and ended it with prayer. Sighing, Lexi got up to get ready and decide which lovely work outfit she would wear. Would it be jeans and flannel or flannel and jeans? Lexi just laughed out loud…she just cracked herself up sometimes!

Lexi pulled up an hour later, and seeing Judd working on the front door she tooted her horn and waved as she rolled to a stop. Judd walked over and opened the door for her, then helped her unload the purchases she had made for the house. Judd just shook his head as he eyed all the light fixtures, cabinet hardware, and samples of paint and tile. She was on a roll and he 'figured' he'd have to roll in her direction.

That thought proved to be a correct assumption as he indeed rolled from one room to another taking direction until she came back to the load bearing wall.

"I really want to open the kitchen up into the dining room Judd, so what can be done?"

Judd looked her squarely in the face and said, "Nothing."

"What exactly does nothing mean?"

Judd thought, 'here we go,' and said, "Nothing means nothing Lexi. I cannot take this wall down at all, or the house will cave in."

Lexi got a bit sassy with Judd saying, "Show me why it can't come down…I need to understand."

So Judd grabbed her hand and pulled her into the backroom to the entrance to the attic. They climbed the steps and he told her to carefully walk where he did so as to not fall through. Lexi did as she was told until she felt something fall on her shoulder, screaming she jumped off the frame onto to the ceiling and fell through landing on her backside. Judd was horrified and screamed to hang on as he ran back down the steps and found her groaning on the kitchen floor.

"Lexi…are you hurt? For heaven's sake, you're just going to have to take my word that I know what I'm doing! If I say a wall can't come down, I have my reasons…okay?"

Lexi looked up into Judd's eyes trying hard to focus but the pain was shooting down her leg. She groaned as he helped her up and sat her in the rocker. Dusting her off and pulling sheetrock out of her hair, did not deter his continued scolding.

Finally, Lexi looked back at him and said, "If you're through fussing at me, I will tell you that I need to lie down somewhere."

With one quick swoop of his arms he picked her up and headed out the door.

"What are you doing Judd Taylor? I meant lie down on the floor somewhere."

"No, you're going to lie down at my house until I see that you'll be alright," and with a quick firm look at her, she closed her mouth and held on tight.

"Well that was a first," he thought to himself.

Judd was absolutely furious with himself for not hanging on to her. She could have seriously been hurt and that would have killed him. But, sometimes she made him absolutely crazy with her questioning his decision, when he knew what was best…at least with a load-bearing wall that is.

He laid Lexi down on the sofa and told her not to move as he grabbed a blanket and tucked it in around her. Every time she tried to say something, he hushed her as he rushed around the kitchen pouring her a glass of water and grabbing the Ibuprofen bottle. Judd sat beside her and held out the water and pills to take. As she started to protest, he shook his head but Lexi blurted out, "Judd, if you don't let me tell you that I have to go to the bathroom, your sofa is going to be ruined!"

Judd quickly got up and helped her to the bathroom where she gasped when she looked in the mirror. Her hair was full of dust and dirt, her shirt was torn, mascara under her eyes and her jean pocket was ripped. Borrowing Judd's comb and dousing her face with water, she did the best she could and ended up tying her shirt at the waist to hide the rip.

Judd waited patiently at the door then escorted her back to the sofa where she took her pills without question. That was a first, he thought.

Lexi sat back on the sofa and smiled at Judd wondering why on earth he never married. He was kind, thoughtful, interesting, funny, maddening, and quite handsome in her opinion. Judd on the other hand was thinking how much she drove him senseless…he lost all reason when he was around her. How could a woman so little occupy his mind at all times?

"Judd, thank you for taking such good care of me," Lexi said.

Judd leaned in toward her face and said, "You're welcome," then hesitated for a split second before lightly kissing her. Pulling back he looked for answers to his unasked questions. She pulled him closer answering all questions with a long passionate kiss. Judd gathered his long ago princess into his arms and they hobbled back down to the farmhouse to continue the flip. And after that? Well, what usually happens when a childhood prince marries his childhood princess? They live happily ever after...

"A sweet friendship refreshes the soul."
Proverbs 27:9

A Little Dirt Never Hurt Anyone

Hattie shifted her small frame from the left hip to the right as she looked out the window. "There he goes again," she whispered. "Mama's gonna get nervous seeing him prance around like that." Charming, the family horse had begun to move with the choir's singing and gospel praising. It was a common occurrence, and he had quite the reputation for being a good-natured soul. Hattie didn't know if horses could be Christians but, if so, he was a good one.

Anne, (with an 'e') leaned toward her daughter to see what she was whispering about. Anne's eyes lit up with a smile before it hit her lips as she watched Charming prance. It was a sight for sore eyes to see such a large animal sway to God's melodies, although it did make her a bit jittery on the buggy ride back home.

Running her hand over her dress to straighten out a few wrinkles, Anne closed her eyes for the benediction. The air was thick and her face was beginning to glisten with drops of perspiration, making her restless to get outside in the breeze. The church had been looking for a new preacher for months and it seemed every Sunday brought a new face, a longer prayer, and an increase in temperature. Hattie squirmed beside her, finally dashing outside as the preacher said, "Amen."

Outside, both mother and daughter inhaled the cooler air. Anne checked Charming's bridle and made sure the buggy was secure. "C'mon young lady," she called to Hattie. "Let's get home for lunch." Hattie climbed in and sat beside her mother.

Anne was young and quite lovely to look at. Only 24, she was raising her four-year old daughter alone. She was not married, and when her parents had discovered her dilemma four years ago, they'd sent her to the North. Their instructions had been clear – leave the newborn with another family before returning home.

Anne looked over at Hattie's tiny face framed with auburn ringlets, her eyes a copper color with golden flecks. She had very unusual coloring for a child. She was delightful and had a heart to love people. Give her away? Absolutely not. Anne was her mother and that would be how it stood. After her birth, Anne packed up their clothes to start a new life. She'd been somewhat educated, her parents had made sure of that, and she was also very well trained in etiquette, dance and stitching. Now she'd see if any of those learning experiences could help her make money.

Sighing, Anne jerked the reins and Charming started his infamous prance. Anne giggled to herself. Charming was her Prince for now, and Hattie her princess.

She was content.

Anne steered the buggy to the boarding house where she'd lived the past four years. It was leaning toward the shabby side, but always clean. As the owner, Mrs. Hawkins said, "Just because you may not have much, don't mean you couldn't be clean." So clean they were, that is until a stranger came to town late last night and rented a room next to Anne's. Earlier that morning, she and Hattie passed him on the stairs…gazing just long enough to assess him properly. He seemed to be in his late twenties, with a might dirty face to match his layer upon layer of dirty clothes. Amazingly, his teeth were straight and white and his eyes were clear, almost see-through blue, with hair dark as molasses. Hmmm, Anne thought, maybe after a bath he'd live up to those fine features God gave him.

After arriving home from church, Anne began to put lunch on the table when she turned too quickly bumping into the handsome stranger.

"Excuse me sir," Anne spoke softly.

"My fault," he said grinning as if he was enjoying the moment.

Hattie, who had been clinging to her mother peeked out from behind her skirt and wrinkled her cute nose to the smell of manly sweat.

Anne reading the signs, quickly tried to shush her before any embarrassing words came out, but…..too late.

"Mister," Hattie called out.

"Mister," she repeated.

The dirty Mr. Brownlow turned around to the little girl and bent down to her level.

"Yes," he replied.

Hattie quickly stuck out her hand and introduced herself saying, "Welcome Sir. I'm Hattie." Mr. Brownlow smiled and said, "How do you do little Hattie?"

Hattie grinned saying, "I'm doing well but you're really dirty…you need a bath!"

Anne gasped and Mr. Brownlow roared.

"I do indeed," he said. "I've been traveling dusty roads for a couple of weeks…so, I am a bit filthy. Would you happen to know where I could take one?"

"Why in your room, of course." And with that Hattie whirled around distracted by a dog barking outside. Mr. Brownlow's eyes traveled up to Anne's eyes with much approval and tipped his hat goodbye.

Anne looked down and spun herself out of sight. A bit breathless and put out with herself. He was just a man traveling through town… no need to be captivated by a smile that was not likely to stay around. Besides, she had Hattie and Charming…who needed a man who probably didn't know manners or even have a Bible. Not her!

Anne got ready for her Monday class which she held in the parlor. She taught intricate stitches and techniques that most girls didn't learn from their busy mothers, she taught proper etiquette and at every opportunity she talked about Jesus and His love for them. She wanted so much for the girls, especially in the area of marriage. She desired that each girl's heart should be so lost in God that a man would have to seek Him to find her. She wanted that for herself…and she knew God gave second chances, and devoutly prayed for one.

Anne was pondering on the scripture she wanted the girls to embroider along with a couple of fancy rose techniques, when she stumbled over a few buckets of steaming hot water in the kitchen. Apparently, Mrs. Hawkins was busy helping Mr. Brownlow prepare for his bath.

"Oh, so glad you are here Anne, could you help me tote these buckets to Mr. Brownlow's room please?"

Startled, Anne muttered, "yes," and picked up two following her to his door.

"Mr. Brownlow, we're here with your bath water."

Opening the door, Mr. Brownlow stood in his pants, undershirt and bare feet. Anne caught her breath and looked at the floor wishing it would just open up and swallow her. Oh, why was she feeling like this?

"You have met Anne, haven't you Mr. Brownlow" said Ms. Hawkins.

Mr. Brownlow looked at Anne with eyes that speared her soul, and said, "Well, I've met Hattie, but haven't had the official pleasure of her mother." He said with a dimpled grin.

"Oh my word, she thought...why did he have to have such charming dimples?"

Not one to reveal her thoughts, Anne looked at him squarely and replied, "Very nice to meet you." And with that she sat the buckets at his dirty feet with water sloshing out onto his toes.

"Please call me Hutch," he said.

"Thank you," and turned rather awkwardly and walked out thinking she heard him chuckle as he shut the door.

The next morning Anne prepared for the day by grabbing her Bible and heading to the parlor for a few minutes of quiet time with the Lord. As she walked in she was met with a smile as Hutch rose to his feet to greet her.

"Hello Anne," he said as he nodded to a chair he held out.

"Good morning Hutch," she said and thanked him for the seat.

Anne pulled out her Bible and began to read. Out of the corner of her eye she noticed that he also had his Bible opened.

No words were needed...for she hid this moment in her heart.

The days passed quickly and each morning she was met by Hutch, always the gentleman and each day within minutes they would have a lively discussion about the scripture. What a joy each day was, what a blessing to get to know such a man. But, other than those discussions, she had not learned why exactly he was here. Anne was reluctant to ask fearing he would feel it an invasion to his privacy.

Everywhere Hutch went he made friends quickly, and Hattie was no exception...she was his shadow and he adored her. Even Charming pranced just a little when Hutch passed humming his gospel tunes.

Saturday morning came and Anne was once again getting ready to teach her girls when Hutch stopped her in the hall and asked if she would like to take a walk in the cool air.

"Well, my girls will be here soon," she stammered.

"It won't take long Anne, I just would like to ask you a question."

Anne nodded and followed his lead.

A few moments later, Hutch stopped and leaned against a tree looking directly into her eyes as he asked the question.

"Anne would you mind telling me about Hattie? Is there a husband?"

Anne looked down at her hands, allowing tears to swallow her eyes. She struggled to gain control of her emotions before looking directly at Hutch feeling the tears trickle down.

"No, there is no husband, and never has been." Anne groped for the appropriate words to explain. "When I was nineteen, I went for a walk not far from home when I was attacked, robbed of my jewelry and beaten for trying to get him off of me. It was a couple of months later that I discovered I was with child. My parents sent me away to avoid disgrace, and wanted me to give my baby away and come home. I could not do it. So, after Hattie was born, I packed up and moved here to make a new life."

Anne didn't think she even breathed while telling him and Hutch just watched taking in her every word. He reached for her hand trying to control his own emotions, "Anne, you are a very special and coura-geous woman, thank you for telling me."

Hutch's heart broke for the terrifying attack she endured. He looked at her petite frame, barely five feet tall, with auburn hair swept up in a loose bun with a few stray wisps framing her lovely face. He could barely keep from holding her, protecting her from further hurt. They walked back in silence to the boarding house where Anne's students were waiting.

In his room, Hutch grabbed his Bible praying for guidance, for his heart was going where he never dreamed it could.

Sunday tiptoed in before Anne realized it was upon her. Dressed and ready, she waited for Hattie to finish putting on her shoes. She was so proud that she could do it by herself. They finally headed out the door to hitch up Charming to the buggy and make way for church. She looked around for Hutch and was disappointed when she didn't see him.

"C'mon Charming," Anne crooned softly, "Today is the Lord's Day, and you get to sway to the music." She patted his neck, then helped Hattie into the buggy before grabbing the reins.

Anne and Hattie arrived, got Charming settled at the hitching post, and walked in greeting friends as they moved towards the front sitting in their usual pew. While waiting for the sermon, Anne opened her Bible for the day's scripture when she heard a familiar voice.

"Today is the Day the Lord has made, let us rejoice and be glad in it," Hutch spoke with joyful authority looking directly at Anne.

Anne gasped letting her Bible fall to the floor making a loud thud. Hattie scooted to retrieve it saying, "Mama, there's Mister Hutch....is HE the preacher?"

Anne's face drained of all blood and nodded yes. Hutch contin-ued on preaching God's word like she had never heard before. The two hours flew quickly by, even Charming seemed surprised and a little more 'spirited' when they went outside after the benediction.

Hutch walked up to Anne and gently grabbed her face in his hands... "Marry me, Anne...I have loved you from the moment you sloshed wa-ter on my toes and Hattie captured my heart telling me I needed a bath."

"You mean I'll be a pastor's wife? And are you the new permanent preacher?"

"Yes and yes," Hutch whispered.

"And Hattie?" Anne continued... "What about Hattie?"

Hutch kissed her softly and said, "She already has my heart, do I have yours?"

Anne raised her lovely glowing face to his and said, "Yes."

Charming must have heard gospel singing, because he started swaying...

And Hattie? Well, she was just happy....

"Clothe yourselves with compassion, kindness, humility, gentleness and patience." Colossians 3:12

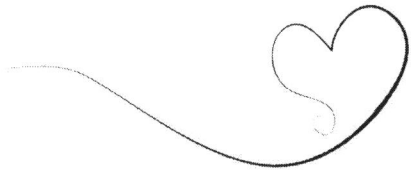

Open Your Heart

Sinking into the feather mattress Lorrie felt the coolness of her grandmother's cotton sheets against her skin. The window had been raised allowing the breeze to pull in the fresh fragrances of the wild roses hanging over the wrought iron fence. Pulling the sheet up to her chin Lorrie observed the room taking in the time-honored furnishings. The oak bed with the large round four poster spindles, the dresser with the simple round mirror that her mother gazed into many a day as she got ready for school. The drawers full of memories like her mom hiding a chocolate bar from her sisters and just taking a bite once a day relishing the sweetness of chocolate. She soaked in the familiar feeling safe, secure and happy.

At six o'clock the alarm went off, and Lorrie hears Nana pushing the off button and creeping quietly out of bed. In her mind she sees Nana turning and yanking the bed sheets up tucking them under the pillow, she quickly pushed all the wrinkles out before pulling up the chenille bedspread. In Nana's eyes everything was done hastily …raising five kids had dictated high speed. By seven, the smell of biscuits, sausage and country gravy trickled into her room pulling Lorrie out of bed. She grinned to herself as she looked over her childhood room, the one where she visited with cousins and dreamt up spectacular dreams. Lorrie smiled over those thoughts as she put her feet on the chilly wood floors, made up the bed, and pulled on her well-loved housecoat.

"Well good morning Lorrie-Belle," she said while flipping the sausage. She always added the 'Belle' to her name even though she was just plain old Lorrie and…truly wouldn't have it any other way. Grabbing her grandmother around the waist she gave her a quick hug before sitting down to feast on more childhood memories. The only thing that was different was the coffee she now added to the meal...caffeine was definitely a part of her life now.

Lorrie smiled to herself while looking around the countertops laced with pounds of flour, sugar and cornmeal tied up in loaf bread bags to keep the 'mealy bugs' away. Her gaze went to the top of the old white fridge where a square glass jar held soft peppermint sticks given out when asked. As Lorrie ate, they reminisced over family gatherings and always, always discussed spiritual things. She loved her Nana and relished the rare times she got to spend with her.

"Lorrie-Belle, you're going to be late for your appointment," she admonished.

"Oops, you're right," she replied.

Quickly, she got up and ran to her room to get ready for the interview in downtown Atlanta. It was an amazing opportunity and was not only surprised but delighted to be asked to interview for one of the writer's position on a Christian Network. Lorrie's head spun for days as she pondered this opportunity. She couldn't help but to dream of doors being opened and her talent being 'discovered'.

Nana yelled out a prayer as she scurried to her car. Waving out the window Lorrie called out, "keep praying for me!"

Turning off of Peachtree Street, she headed to Oak Haven Drive surprised that it led to a residential area. Turning into the driveway of an old Atlanta home, red brick with white antebellum columns beckoned her to the front door, and she knocked a little hesitantly.

The door opened and a big bright smiled greeted her...dimples and all.

"Welcome! I'm Angel...half owner of this network but, she whispered, I'm the most important half," and with that she giggled as she let me in.

"Why, you aren't bigger than a minute! Come on in and let me pull out something fattening to eat before we get started. Besides if I pull it out, then I can eat it too without the guilt from my husband's eagle eye watching me." Angel chuckled to herself as she pulled a delicious looking coffee cake topped with cranberries and walnuts. Slicing two large pieces onto some lovely white ironstone she also poured two steaming cups of coffee and sat down.

"Now Lorrie," Angel said, "I have your portfolio which, I must say, is quite impressive with all the accomplishments you have achieved in the Christian realm. But, what I want to know at the moment, is your personal testimony."

Lorrie looked up quite surprised at her request. "You want my testimony?"

"Why yes dear, your writings show your heart and your depth, but I want to know your beginning."

Lorrie pondered for just a moment before speaking.

"I didn't have a lightning bolt moment Angel, my love for the Lord came softly in baby steps. It kept evolving after I accepted Christ in my heart as a young teen. Then life began to happen…I married, had a baby and all was amazing. I had loved this man since I was fifteen, but he and my daughter were killed in a car accident. I survived…why, I don't know. My heart died that moment and I've struggled to go on. One thing I do know, there will never be another man that I could love as much as I loved Lance…nor, could I love a daughter as much as I loved Lily Rose. She was a breathtakingly beautiful baby that stole my heart forever." Lorrie didn't realize that tears had filled not only her eyes but Angel's.

"I knew there was a reason for the depth of your writing, only souls that have experienced such sorrow can truly write the way you do." Angel said leaning back in her chair, her cake unattended as she pondered what to do. She had never hired anyone without the mutual consent of her husband and son, they were a team…but, she had never felt so compelled to hire someone on the spot as she did Lorrie. Not quite understanding fully why, she leaned in and asked her, "I want you on our writing team, would you consider it?"

Lorrie sucked in her breath. "Would she?"

Lorrie heard the words "yes" come out of her mouth.

Angel leaned over and hugged her. "Welcome to the team!" she exclaimed.

Lorrie looked up and asked, "Who all is on the team?"

Angel just laughed and winked, "Just my son, Jake."

"Jake Sebastian? " Lorrie inquired.

"Now don't you worry Lorrie, Jake is an amazing writer and y'all will make a great team."

Lorrie was a bit dazed. Jake Sebastian was well known in the Christian writing domain, and she was going to be his partner?" She was overwhelmed with intimidation...

Angel patted her hand, "Lorrie, you still with me?"

Lorrie laughed, "I'm still here just a bit dazed to be working with your son."

"Oh, now don't let that intimidate you, he's just an everyday kind of fella...that puts his pants on the same way as everybody else. Although, she laughed, he does tend to get a bit big for his britches on occasion and I just have to make him take out his mama's trash and he calms back down," she said.

Lorrie giggled as she picked up her bag and walked towards the door. Angel followed, giving her another quick hug and said, "Be careful and we'll be in touch soon with all the details and start date."

Cheeks flushed matching her auburn hair, she grabbed her sunglasses from her bag and put them over her greenish gray eyes. Freckles dotted her nose in a cute endearing way especially when she crinkled her nose in laughter. She was definitely a head-turner, with her trim figure sliding into her red convertible, Lorrie felt a bit lightheaded with the job looming over her head. But, driving her little indulgence always seem to calm her nerves and preserve her sanity.

Angel sat back down to finish her cake while she pondered. What would Joe and Jake think about her hiring Lorrie without their input? Both were take-charge kind of men, always wanting to make the final decisions. But, this time Angel felt that God was directing her to hire Lorrie. Well, it was done and the men in her life would just have to trust her.

Later that night, Joe arrived home and called out for Angel, "Honey, I'm home."

Angel came running and hugged her husband of forty years. He was still just as handsome as he was when they married, maybe more so. Silver hair now, but still thick and wavy framing his tanned, leathered skin. His blue eyes were always focused, his mind never stopping. She always wondered why he chose her...he could have had any beautiful woman but she caught his eye. Angel was forever bubbly, loving and giving. She tended to be a bit boisterous and with her big personality came a big appetite which was her downfall. Definitely attractive, she however tended to be a bit thick in the middle, Joe called it love handles on a mission, she called it a plain ole' nuisance. But nevertheless, they had a special love that had endured.

"How was your day, Hon? Anything new to report?

Angel cocked her head in shock. Did he already know and was testing her? But how could he? "Well, she began, I interviewed a woman name Lorrie Taylor Landers. Very talented, very bright and such a delight to talk to.

It was Joe's turn to cock his head on her last comment. "Hmmm, a delight to talk to?" he asked. "Why yes, she was young, about Jake's age, with quite a portfolio to share with me. Her personality was definitely easy."

"So did you think she was hire worthy?"

Angel fidgeted for a moment.

With that tale-tale sign he knew.

"You hired her didn't you?"

"Yes," she said, suddenly confident and decisive, "I did," and waited for a possible raised brow that indicated concern. But no raised brow came.

"Well Honey, after all this time we have done this business together, I'm sure you know what we're looking for...I can't wait to meet her."

Angel was stunned but it didn't keep her from hugging and kissing Joe one more time.

Joe leaned back and said, "I'm the easy one Angel, you still have Jake to tell and I can assure you, he won't like it one bit!"

Angel said, "I'm going to set up a meeting, he will love her…I'm sure of it."

That next day Angel called Lorrie on her cell and set up a lunch meeting with her and Jake. She felt like they would do best without her along. All she told Jake was she wanted his input on Lorrie, she felt like she was perfect for the job.

Jake's casual dress was always with good taste. His good looks mimicked his dad's. Jake inherited his Dad's light blue eyes that stood out against his thick dark hair. His mom was not thrilled with his stubble-like beard but she loved his personality which happened to be much like hers. Jake had been blessed with a keen talent for words and plots. As a Christian, he valued the family, morals and encouragement to do the right thing. Their network was called appropriately, "Family."

He looked forward to the lunch meeting with Lorrie Landers, as his mom spoke highly of her and he was anxious to meet with her. Although, he was a bit concerned that her abilities were in writing and not necessarily script writing. But, that could be taught to the right person.

Lorrie changed her clothes four times. What do you wear to meet the man you are going to work with daily on a one-to-one basis? She could just hear her Nana say, "Goodness Lorrie-Belle, just wear what is comfortable to you…he's only going to stare at your eyes anyway." Lorrie grinned at that because she always told Lorrie she had eyes that could melt a man's heart. They did one time, but she could not fathom another man in her life.

Lorrie shook her head to empty her thoughts and decided on the green fitted dress, simple but classic, one of those that never went out of style. She wore high heeled sandals and carried the latest in burlap bags. Checking her make-up one more time before putting on her sun glasses she headed out to meet Jake at a place called, Magnolia Leaf, a new lunch restaurant not far from the Family Network office.

Angel had instructed Lorrie to give the hostess her name and she would direct her to Jake's table. Upon arriving, Lorrie walked in with confidence she really did not possess and gave her name. Jake happened to look up at the same moment she entered the room. "Wow," he thought, "that woman is lovely."

Jake's eyes grew big as the waiter brought Lorrie to his table and left. Jake quickly stood up and shook her hand. He almost felt like a school boy, sweaty and nervous.

"You must be Lorrie," he said, "I'm Jake Sebastian."

"Yes, I am and so nice to meet you," she replied.

Jake pulled her chair out then sat directly across from her. He smiled as they took a few minutes for small talk. Jake was instantly smitten, a feeling he had not had in many years. She was special...humble, soft-spoken, petite in frame, but there was strength in her character.

It might have made him feel better had he known what Lorrie was thinking. She too, was intrigued with him. She felt her heart leap upon meeting him but she stopped it at that moment, before the guilt set in and stole her joy for the day.

Lorrie drew in her breath and answered his questions easily and with passion. She loved writing! It brought her such joy and came quite naturally. She knew it was because she tried hard to honor God with her words.

Jake asked one more question, "What was your impression of my mother?"

Lorrie leaned back and took a sip of her water before answering. "I loved Angel, she was joyful, compassionate, encouraging and a true cheerleader for her family and business. She was a delight to be with and I especially liked her coffee cake," she said with a grin.

Jake grinned on that last comment. "Yes, my mom does love her cake and without a doubt that put a feather in your cap if you loved it too!"

"So," he continued, "are you interested in working with me?"

Lorrie smiled and nodded her head yes. Her eyes met his for a split second before they shook hands and he brought out the contract to go over and sign. Within another hour, they had completed the paperwork and all that was left was the start date.

"How about next Monday? That should give you time to prepare some ideas for our next movie set for a year from now. We're focusing on a love story that involves some very unique plots that haven't been done before. We will start at 9:00 a.m. at the house in our office, off the kitchen. We never did move our offices to a regular office park because we were so comfortable in our home. Hopefully, this will be alright for you?"

"Absolutely," she said. "Do you live there also?" she inquired.

Laughing out loud he replied, "You got me with that one, and no I do not. I haven't lived with my parents since high school. I moved out from college dorm life into an apartment and have been on my own since. How about you?"

Lorrie squirmed for just a moment reluctant to give her life story so soon. "I live alone in a house in the suburbs, about twenty minutes north from here." Jake smiled sensing she was uncomfortable talking about herself and asked for the check. Lorrie picked up her purse to pay half but Jake waved her off. "Not this time Lorrie…you can pick up the check when we go to a more expensive restaurant," he said laughing. Lorrie giggled too, she enjoyed his banter.

Monday came quickly and Lorrie reported to work at 9:00 a.m. sharp. Jake was already there drinking coffee and typing on his laptop. Looking up, he motioned for her to sit down. Dressed casual in skinny pants and cream lace top layered with tasteful jewelry, she looked fabulous. Lorrie worried that she was way too casual but Jake had insisted it was that kind of working atmosphere.

Their discussion began and not without laughter as they teased over how a romance should go, what would be involved, and who was going to be the difficult person, the man or woman. That definitely kept the conversation flowing. Before long, Angel appeared by poking her head in the door.

"What's all the talking about? Y'all haven't stopped since this morning and now its two o'clock…any progress?"

Jake leaned back in his chair and said, "Mom…we have a romance that revolves around flipping houses. As far as I know, this scenario has never been done on any network. Angel pondered on that a moment and said, "go for it, write the script and let's see where it goes."

Jake winked at his mom before she turned and left. Lorrie noticed the wink and tucked that into her heart to recall later. A son that treats his mom with love and respect will do the same for a wife. Lance had been like that, he would have liked Jake.

After a late lunch, they hammered out some more. Lorrie thought the roles should change up a bit and maybe make the woman the contractor who, in the end, fell in love with the nosey neighbor who insisted on giving her advice. Jake pondered on that and thought they should explore that idea. Wrapping up the day, Jake grinned at Lorrie saying, "great day Lorrie, I'll see you tomorrow."

Lorrie picked up her bag and headed out the door. She felt light, almost care-free...it had been a great day. Now if she could just keep Jake out of her thoughts.

Jake went into the kitchen and sat down at the table. He stretched out his legs and then ran his hand through his hair. Angel knew what that meant...she had seen it a few times and it always involved a girl that was on his mind.

"How did the day go, Jake?" Angel asked.

"It was really good, Mom, and as you said, she is quite talented. I love the ideas she came up with and I think we're a good fit."

"Really?" his mom said.

Jake looked up at his mom and grinned. "I know what 'really' means and I'm not going there."

"Hmmm...you're attracted to her aren't you Jake?"

Jake just grabbed his coat, gave his mom a kiss on the cheek and left, feeling upbeat. He knew he was attracted to her, but they worked together. He had to be very careful with this situation.

The next day, Lorrie walked in with fresh ideas for the plot and the debate begin. She could tell that he loved the deliberation as much as she did. Before long, it was lunch and she stood up and stretched a little.

Jack said, "How about lunch at the little café around the corner?"

"Wonderful, I'll drive," Lorrie said.

"Well, I like that…" he said grinning.

He climbed into her sporty red convertible, thinking this car showed a definite fun side. They were chatting the few minutes it took to get to the restaurant when out of nowhere a moving truck turned the corner coming into her lane and slammed into the side of her car. Lorrie screamed as the air bag ejected.

Jake jumped into action, as he was not hurt, just a bit dazed. He opened his door and ran around to Lorrie's side, opening her door and pulling her out. She was sobbing as she clung to him. Jake tried to put her down so he could make sure she wasn't hurt but she wouldn't let go. The man driving the moving truck ran over to see if they were alright. Jake nodded yes and asked him to call 911 for the police. The man walked off pulling out his cell phone.

"Lorrie," Jake whispered, "It's alright, I promise," he murmured in her ear. The more he tried to soothe, the more she cried. He just could not figure it out.

In her sobs, he heard her moan the words, 'Lily Rose,' and later when she was in more control he asked who Lily Rose was?

"My daughter. She was a little over a year old when my husband, Lance and I were taking our Lily Rose to the park when a man pulled out in a Moving Van going at a high speed. Lance didn't have time to react and we were hit. Both my husband and daughter died instantly, while I was hardly hurt."

Jake gathered her back in her arms as the tears poured down again. Now he understood everything…

After the report was completed, the police dropped them off at the house as the car had to be towed. Lorrie was quiet, and from the looks of her she was exhausted emotionally.

Jake took her back to the guest room and insisted she lay down for a while. She didn't protest much…the memories were too raw at the moment. He covered her up with a light blanket and closed the door.

Angel came over and hugged her son. Giving his mom a kiss he sat down for coffee. "Mom, did you know about Lorrie's husband and daughter?" he asked.

"Yes, she shared with me the day I hired her."

"Why didn't you tell me?" Jake looked demanding at his mother.

"It wasn't my story to tell; Lorrie needed to tell you when she wanted you to know."

Jake quickly looked apologetic and said, "Oh, I see...that makes sense."

Later Jake took Lorrie home and saw her into her home. It was very comfortable with a Farmhouse feel. He liked that. Jake was tired of the modern look his female friends had...this was a bright, cheerful loving home. He really hated to leave her.

Lorrie thanked him with a hug and apologized one more time for breaking down and clinging to him for so long. Jake shook his head and said, "Lorrie, let it go, I'm just glad I was with you..."

Jake walked back to the front door and then for some reason leaned over and kissed her cheek. Lorrie just stared as he turned and left. "Oh no," she thought, "I just can't have feelings for him, he is my boss and in my heart, I'm still married." With a groan, Lorrie fell on the sofa and relived her day. Jake did just what Lance would have done...he comforted her, held her...took care of her and shielded her.

She was undone, and she knew it.

***

Jake got back to his loft apartment and pulled on his sweats. He also plopped down on his sofa exhausted from the day's events. He felt sad for Lorrie with the loss of her family. It must have been so terribly difficult for her. Then he agonized that he had feelings for her, what would or should he do with those?

Lorrie woke the next morning, her eyes slowly opened kicking her brain into recalling the previous day's events. She was mortified that she had lost control, it had been several years since she had sobbed like that for Lance and Lily Rose. It felt good to release.

She quickly dressed in jeans and a shirt, pulled on her boots and headed out just in time to realize she didn't have a car...however, there was one in her driveway. Walking closer she noticed a note on the windshield. "We had an extra car for you to use until yours is fixed." Lorrie's eyes filled with tears...Jake hardly knew her, but he continued to shield her from any stress.

Lorrie got in the car and promptly called her Nana telling her all the events of the last several days. Nana listened quietly and then said, "Lorrie, God is taking care of you...don't miss His blessing...have an open heart and open arms to receive."

Lorrie smiled to herself, "Nana, you're such the romantic."

"Well, land sakes honey, my body is a bag full of sags but my heart is just as young as yours. God is giving you love again...embrace it."

Lorrie pondered on her Nana's words while driving, not quite sure what to do or say when she arrived at work with Jake. She prayed for direction.

She walked into the house and met Angel in the hall where she got a huge bear hug.

"How about something to eat...cures everything," she said with a grin.

"Sure Angel, maybe something little." Lorrie walked around the table and cut a slice of fresh apple bread and grabbed a cup of coffee.

"Hmmm...smells good Angel."

"What smells good," Jake said rounding the corner.

Lorrie's heart leaped into her throat.

Jake grabbed the bread and coffee his mom handed him and went into the office. Lorrie did the same.

Jake sat at the desk and thought for just a moment before saying, "Lorrie, would you mind sharing your story about your family...start at the beginning."

Lorrie leaned back and began with how she and Lance met, married and was blessed with Lily Rose...the love of her life. She felt her face grow moist from the tears that trickled down her cheeks, sweet memory tears this time. She even pulled out their last family picture she kept in her wallet. After a while, Jake got up, walked around his desk and pulled her close, Lorrie didn't resist.

"Is there room in your heart for me Lorrie?"

She didn't speak…her heart was too full, instead she leaned in and kissed him.

Jake looked into her eyes and said, "I take that as a yes."

"Oh, yes…there is room."

Jake leaned in this time and kissed her lips…her arms wrapped around his, forgetting entirely about work.

For just a second Lorrie thought of her Nana's words "Open heart, open arms."

"You were right Nana," she thought. "So, so right."

"Be the light." Matthew 5:14

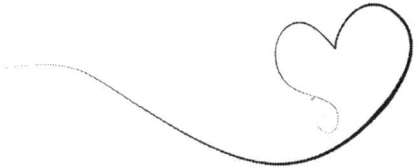

Honey-Bee Pleased

Honestly, you would think we were thirteen years old!" Hope said giggling as she swatted at a fly with her hand.

"Oh shoot, I missed"

Grace just grinned as she rolled her eyes at her 'twinsie' as they called each other. Actually, they weren't twins, but cousins connected in a very special way. Their mothers were sisters that went into labor on the same day, labored in the same room, and delivered Hope and Grace just two hours apart!

Thus began a special relationship that delighted their grandmother, Honey-Bee. Now, Honey-Bee was short in stature, or as the country folk would say, "low to the ground," She was a plump, sassy, determined woman that always had her say.and usually got her way. But, oh, what a soft spot she had for her grand-girls, Hope and Grace. They were her heart and she told them so, daily. She would always say to them, "Oh, Honey-be good or Honey-be happy, or Honey-behave and so Honey-Bee she became and wore her name proudly.

The girls spent their summers at the farmhouse helping Honey-Bee can the vegetables they raised in the garden. They took care of the chickens throwing feed out and secretly named two of them Prissy and Prude. Hope and Grace were taught all the embroidery stitches and became quite creative with their work. And, as the sun went down Honey-Bee would have them all on the porch drinking ice tea and telling stories of the depression years. Hope was especially fascinated one night when Honey-Bee told of not having any elastic to make her daughters the underwear they desperately needed. But, the Good Lord gave her the idea of taking the inner-tubing out of an old bicycle tire and cutting into strips that worked nicely to stretch the waistbands. In their minds, Honey-Bee was the smartest woman who ever lived...

Their summers each year were priceless and never did they miss a one until they graduated from college...where both took jobs in the field they chose. Hope was Interior Design and Grace was Landscaping. Honey-Bee was not a bit surprised, after all, they did learn from the best or so they told her, she thought grinning to herself.

Six years later, Honey-Bee, the stubborn woman that she was, kept refusing help from anyone. She was only ninety in spirit, her body and mind were just fine and thank you, she would say. But, she fell toting wood onto the porch and never recovered. The girls visited and pampered their dear Honey-Bee, but she would just pat their hands and say, 'today may be my Glory day...I'm ready."

Just a few days later she was gone.

The girls were devastated. They spent several days hanging out at the farmhouse they so dearly loved, laughing, reliving summers with Honey-Bee, sharing her stories and of course, swatting flies and being silly.

Hope leaned back in her rocker and said to Grace, "What do you suppose will happen to the farm? Do you think our moms will sell it?"

Grace blinked back sudden tears at the thought, "Oh Hope, you don't really think they would sell, do you?"

"I don't know," she said sadly, "I can't imagine that they would but you know our moms are city girls and they wouldn't move out this far."

"But, it's not that far," Grace whined. "I mean we're only a couple of miles from town and they have some really neat restaurants and shops. I just can't imagine not coming here anymore, it would just kill me!" and with that statement Grace got out of her rocker and flopped back on the bed.

Sitting at the old wooden kitchen table of Honey-Bee's the daughters were sipping coffee as they looked over the will she had left her girls. Susan, the oldest and the mother to Hope began to read it out loud to Beth, the mother to Grace.

"Hmmm, Beth, mom says here that the farmhouse is to go to both the girls as their inheritance, and you and I are to receive most of the furnishings and all of her financial assets."

Beth looked up and smiled, "Mom sure did love our girls, didn't she Sis?"

Susan reached over and patted her hand in agreement, "She sure did and the girls will be thrilled!"

But, what do you suppose they will do with this place? Beth pondered for a moment.

Susan got up and called upstairs to the girls, "Hope and Grace come down for a few minutes please, we have some news to share."

Susan looked over at Beth and said, "I think we're fix'n to find out."

Hope and Grace looked at each other as they scrambled to put on their flip-flops and run down the steps. You would never know they were both 28 years old and professionals, for at the moment they looked like curious teenagers.

"What's up Mom?" said Hope to Susan.

"Well, your aunt and I were going over Honey-Bee's will and apparently she has left you and Grace with a great deal of responsibility.

"What kind of responsibility Aunt Susan?" said Grace.

"Why don't you girls sit down and have a cup of coffee, because we have a lot to talk about."

Several hours later, Hope and Grace wandered back up to the room they had shared each summer and plopped down on their beds in squeals.

"I can't believe she left us the Farmhouse Grace! We never have to lose it!"

"I know, but what in the world are we going to do with it? How can we keep it up when we live and work in the city?"

"I'm not sure, but as Honey-Bee always said, the Good Lord knows the plan, we just got to be listening for it."

"So as sure as Honey-Bee was given the idea for the elastic, the girls were given the plan for the farmhouse, it would become a Bed & Breakfast Inn!"

A few months later, Hope & Grace loaded up a couple of trucks for hauling and headed north to finally live in the farmhouse. They had worked out notices for their jobs, sold condos, and Hope traded in her sports car for a sturdy jeep.

It had taken almost a year of preparation to get the house in shape for guests. They also had to add additional bathrooms to the bedrooms, and update the kitchen a bit. Doing the renovating was truly an act of love and dedication. Each room held a dear memory of Honey-Bee and those moments were priceless.

But, now it was time to move in and 'git to living' as she would say!

Hope drove one truck and Grace the other. The trucks were big and awkward, but it had to be done. Grace followed her cousin on the highway for an hour before getting off the exit for another twenty minute drive to the farmhouse. Hope was feeling a bit tired and groggy but knew there were no Starbucks for a quick pick-me-up caffeine jolt. Noticing a traffic light was looming upon her, Hope began to put her brakes on due to the weight of the truck…but, should have started a few seconds earlier as she firmly bumped into the car in front of her.

Groaning at the mishap, Hope jumped out, brushing off her white jeans which in all probability was not a good choice to move in, and approached the car. The door opened and out stepped a young man, probably in his thirties, dressed in a suit, tie and really expensive shoes.

"Oh know," she thought, "he's going to let me have it." So, Hope braced for a verbal impact, but none came.

Instead, his stern look softened as he quickly glanced at this very lovely girl and saw that she was nervous.

"I am so very sorry," Hope said. "I tried to stop in time, but the weight of the truck was apparently more than I can handle."

"No harm done, at least nothing that can't be fixed. I'm Jackson

Anderson and you are?"

"Oh, I'm sorry, I'm Hope Taylor, a new resident here in town."

Grace had finally stopped her truck and was by then standing near her cousin.

Grace extended her hand and said, "I'm Grace Watson, her cousin and we'll be living in the farmhouse just up the road."

Jackson once again glanced at another lovely young woman and thought to himself, "I am having a banner day," and smiled.

Even though the day was a cool fall day, the girls melted as they spoke with Jackson a few more minutes before climbing back into their respective trucks, but not before Hope said, "just remember Grace, I hit him first," and laughed.

A few days later, things were coming together. The style was completely farmhouse charm through and through but definitely with a young, fun sense to it. The girls had so much fun pulling it together that they had forgotten to finalize the name of their B & B.

"So, are we on the same page for the name?" Hope asked.

Grace appeared thoughtful and said, "I agree with naming it after our Grandmother…whatever else would this place ever be?

So, "Honey-Bee's Farmhouse Bed & Breakfast Inn" it is," and with a clink of their mason jars full of ice tea they slowly sipped their sweetened brew celebrating the newly christened name.

The next morning the girls were eating breakfast and planning their Open House Party for the next month. Getting on the computer, Grace searched for the best flowers to order and arrange in all the tin pails they had on hand. Hope was searching several sites for burlap, lace and frankly, anything with rust, or chipped paint would be fabulous.

The invitations were next and after much discussion, a hundred were ordered and hopefully would arrive in a few days. Now, to get all the businesses addresses and as many local people as they could find. The more that knew they were there, the more successful the B & B would be.

Grace had her work cut out for her with the design and execution of the landscaping. The yard wasn't too bad, but the last fifteen years of Honey-Bee's life had not been dedicated to the yard. She just wasn't able. It took some time and much, much labor, but when Grace pulled it all together, it truly was stunning. The yard now framed Honey-Bee's home with color and movement.

It was December 10th, and an hour away from when the Christmas Open House would begin. The girls raced around doing last minute things before checking their hair one last time. Hope, the girlie girl of the two had long bouncy curls of ash blonde hair flowing down her shoulders. She had tried on several outfits but the winter white lace dress won out paired with her favorite boots, a coat of red lipstick and gloss on her lips and she was stunning. Grace, the more outdoorsy girl with spirited auburn hair and swoopy sassy bangs, chose a green dress that flowed flawlessly against her slim figure, choosing cowgirl boots for flair, she was quite the catch.

The party began with ease, everyone that stopped by was full of compliments and good wishes. So many new people to learn and how awesome to make so many new friends. The girls were thrilled as the night came to a close. Picking up dirty dishes and napkins the girls were full of chatter when the doorbell rang, glancing at the clock, Hope opened the door.

It was Jackson and another Jackson.

Hope was stunned and confused.

"Come on in Jackson and the other Jackson." She said laughing.

He turned to Hope and explained, "This is my identical twin brother Carter, and please forgive us for being so late, but we were delayed in town by clients."

"Clients?" she inquired.

"Yes, we're the Anderson and Anderson Attorneys at law in town."

"Oh my….how wonderful for you two to work together!"

The guys just laughed saying, "Well not sure how wonderful it is but for now it works."

"Where is your other half?" Jackson asked.

Hope called out to Grace who came quickly in the room.

"Hi Jackson, she sang out and then stopped and looked at Hope."

"Which one is Jackson?" she said grinning.

"This one, she said pointing to Jackson and the other is his twin, Carter Anderson."

Carter grabbed Grace's hand and literally felt a mild jolt, he pulled back quickly stunned at himself.

Grace just stared for a moment, mumbled something about dishes and water and excused herself.

The brothers stayed for a little while longer taking the grand tour and promising to send their overnight clients their way.

It was the perfect ending to the perfect night...or almost perfect.

Later, Grace stood at the bathroom sink wondering why she felt so connected to Carter. Why did this feeling disturb/delight her so? She racked her brain, but to no avail.

A few moments more and Hope was at her side. "What was that about Grace? Why did you walk off?"

Grace just shrugged her shoulders and struggled to say the right thing but there was nothing.

Hope just hugged her and went to bed.

Grace tossed and turned that night, finally fully awake at 4 a.m. she threw the covers off and wandered down to the kitchen. She stood at the sink and stared out the window that overlooked the woods. What was it and was Carter feeling the same?

That afternoon Grace and Hope were out raking the front yard, both bundled up but enjoying the exercise when an old friend of Honey-Bee's walked up.

"Well hello ladies," Sally-Sue yelled out.

Both girls ran up and hugged her tight, they hadn't seen Sally-Sue since their grandmother's funeral.

"How are you doing?" the girls asked.

"Mighty fine, I would say," she replied.

She came on in the kitchen and sat for a spell, while the girls poured cream in her cup and then added just a bit of coffee, just the way she liked it....more cream than coffee.

Sally-Sue reminisced for about an hour about this and that through the years when she suddenly was recalling the story about Grace and the snake. "Do you remember that Hon?" she asked.

Grace shook her head no. "What snake?" she asked.

Well, as I remember, you were about five and had wandered off into the woods. You loved the woods and Honey-Bee had a time keeping you out of them. Anyway, you had wandered off and we were looking for you. Even though it was hot, the nights were cool and we were getting scared...you were such a small child.

Unbeknownst to anyone, you had wandered near the creek and disturbed a copperhead, it struck you in the ankle but fortunately you had your rubber boots on and it didn't break your skin, but its fangs were stuck in the rubber. In a panic you started to run, the snake stayed right with you when a young fella was out with his dad shooting his new gun. The dad grabbed you and pulled the snake off and his son quickly shot it dead. When we heard the shot, Honey-Bee ran towards the noise and you flew into her arms sobbing."

Sally-Sue stopped and looked at Grace saying, "You mean you don't remember being traumatized like that?"

Grace looked at her and asked, "Who was the boy that shot the snake, Sally-Sue?"

"Well, I reckon I'm not sure, but I think he was one of the Anderson boys."

That was it...that was Carter, he had saved her.

Grace looked at Hope and smiled...for she knew he was the one. A girl only gets one hero in her life and she met hers at five.

A few nights later Jackson had come by and picked up Hope for dinner and Grace was rocking on the porch in Honey-Bee's favorite chair, it was a comfort thing for Grace to rock to the cadence of the birds singing. Enjoying the night air, she saw Carter drive up and waved. She motioned for him to join her on the porch.

Carter sat on the porch railing and smiled, "You know the last time I saw you, I felt a jolt when I touched you."

Grace smiled and nodded, "Me too, but I didn't know why I felt like I did. It was like we had a connection."

Carter smiled and said, "I was eight and you were five when I heard you scream for help. I ran with my dad towards you when we saw the snake attached to your boot. You were so scared. My dad pulled it off and I shot it. I felt like a hero that day, and I've not experience that feeling since."

"You know, Carter, a girl doesn't get too many heroes in her lifetime…actually one is enough for me."

Carter reached over and took her hand and kissed it…

Jackson and Hope were knee deep in conversation. Hope seemed to soak in every word he said, and Jackson couldn't seem to keep his eyes off hers. She totally fascinated him with her keen sense of style, love for home and family, and she had such a down-home flavor to her personality. He knew the moment she'd 'hit' him on the road, she was the girl for him.

Hope's mind wandered as he spoke thinking of Honey-Bee and how she would like him. He was just the kind of man she would approve of. Good mannered, servant attitude, loved the Lord and was desiring a family life. She desired a life with a man like Jackson but she didn't want to leave out Grace…they were joined at the hip, they were 'twinsie's'.

"Hope?" Jackson grinned as he tried to get her attention.

"Oh, I'm sorry, just thinking about Grace and Honey-Bee."

"What about Grace?" He prodded.

"Oh, I don't know, we're just always together but things could change..." Her thought trailed off.

Jackson clued into her thoughts and winked at Hope, "You know, I think everything is going to be just fine...Carter was headed over to your house after I picked you up, I believe he and Grace are catching up on things about now."

Hope grinned and couldn't wait to get back home.

Six months later, in late spring when the arbor at Honey-Bee's was in full bloom of cascading pink roses, Hope and Grace walked through it and said, "I do," to the men they loved. They were born on the same day, and married the same day...Oh, wouldn't Honey-Bee pleased.

"When you go through deep waters, I will be with you."
Isaiah 43:2

Those Who Wait Upon The Lord...

Picking up her Bible while watching the sunset fade behind the lake, Marcy turned to the scripture about God giving you the 'desires of your heart'...in the stillness of the moment she pondered on those words. Does God really give you the desires of your heart? Marcy was unsure, as she was still single at age 30. Whenever she thought of this, she became overwhelmingly blue...in fact; she thought her name should be Marcy Blue. One of her friends suggested she may need to get new desires, but, Marcy mused...what if God didn't want these for her either. Then what?

Across the lake was a young man, about 32, with reddish brown hair and tender hazel eyes. He, too, had gathered his Bible with a steaming cup of coffee and headed out to the deck to watch the sun make its slow descent.

"Lord," he prayed, "I've tried being patient and wait on your best for me, but I'm lonely...could you hurry up with my bride...please?"

Matthew opened his Bible and read about God giving you the 'desires of your heart' and he held onto those words.

After a while, Matthew went back inside picking up his drawing pad and flipped to the last page to gaze at his sketch. Smiling, he took in the strawberry blonde hair all wispy and wind-blown, her vibrant green eyes and creamy skin that was dotted with just a few well placed freckles. She was lovely, firey and his 'dream girl.'

Matthew looked up towards heaven and said, "Okay God, here she is on paper, where is she for real?"

Marcy woke up late and groaned. Yanking covers off, she jumped up, wincing, as her bare feet hit the cold floors. Flinging on her hot pink bathrobe she turned on her shower waiting for the stream. Later, putting on mascara and dabbing on lip-gloss, Marcy left for her job in town. Social work was rewarding, but on the same hand it certainly pulled at your heartstrings. Just like today, she needed to meet with a new staff attorney to help her with a gut-wrenching case.

Turning into the parking lot she noticed that someone had pulled into her spot, and it had started to rain. After a few minutes of circling the lot, Marcy finally found one on the far end—of course, nowhere near the door. She jumped out, forgetting her umbrella and then locking her keys in the car...Marcy moaned in frustration; sprinting towards the door, her clothes soaked, hair plastered, mascara running and probably late for her meeting.

Trying to open the door with wet hands she managed to slip-in unnoticed until her foot hit the damp floor. Legs flying, arms flailing and BOOM, her bottom and pride hit the floor at the same time! Looking up she stared into the handsome face of...

"Hi," he said, extending his hand to help her up, "Were the close-up parking spaces all taken? I happened to get one next to the door."

Looking at him through wet-yucky hair, her eyes narrowed and a blaze of fire shot out-

"You...you spot stealer," she stuttered, "now, I'm a wet mess." Embarrassed at her outburst Marcy marched off before he could apologize or introduced himself.

Locking herself in the bathroom she managed to fluff-dry her hair, re-do her make-up and stand in front of the hand-dryer until her clothes perked up. Looking at her watch, she panicked at the fast approaching 9:00 a.m. meeting with the new attorney. Grabbing her papers off her desk, she hurried to his office. Knocking, she entered-shock immediately registered on her face as she looked into the handsome face of the man she'd earlier blasted.

"Good morning," he said, feeling his chest tighten as he gazed at her face. "I'm sorry for taking what I now know was an assigned space."

"Hi," she spoke weakly, "and I'm sorry for losing my temper."

74

He stood and walked around his desk offering his had, "My name is Matthew-Matthew Blue," as he looked into the face of his "dream girl"... fiery and lovely and no longer on paper.

"I'm Marcy," she said shaking his hand "knowing" that she would never be blue again-or would she?

One year later...

Matthew and Marcy Blue were cooing with their newborn daughter, Bonnie-Bell Blue who was conceived while honeymooning in the Blue Ridge Mountains at the famous Bluebell Farm Bed & Breakfast.

Who says God doesn't hear the desires of your heart...even the blue ones!

"Kind words are like honey, sweet to the soul and
healthy for the body." Proverbs 16:24

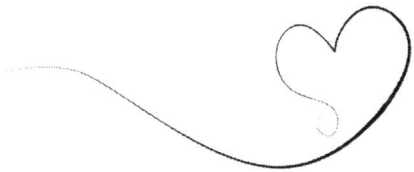

Not In My Plans....

Walking into the dimly lit house, Luke and his real estate agent Tom looked through the shadows while allowing their eyes to focus on the rooms. They found them to be quaint while being rustic in a manly sort of way, with original wood plank floors and bead board ceilings. "So far, so good," thought Luke. Not afraid of a little remodeling, Luke welcomed a challenge and felt an eagerness to continue through the home. The kitchen was a nice size with painted cabinets some inserted with old bubble glass that gave the room tremendous charm. This home suited him, and after a long discussion with Tom, decided to put in an offer.

Luke said his goodbyes, and walked outside examining the fairly large yard one more time. Well maintained, with a cottage feel. Made him think of his grandmother's home and he could almost smell the freshly cut grass mingled with the sweet smell of her roses. Luke laughed at himself getting so sentimental…he better watch it or he'd be way too soft on his students.

With that thought, Luke remembered that he wanted to tour the high school in town where he had accepted a new position as a History and Bible teacher at Oak Mountain Christian School in the hills of North Georgia. He had taken a walk with the principal through all the sections of the school, but he felt a slow, methodical tour by himself would be beneficial to calming his anxious spirit. But, he would do that tomorrow, first he needed to eat somewhere in town and reassess his decision of buying the home.

Luke settled in at the small café facing Main Street drinking coffee while waiting on the Reuben sandwich he'd ordered. He figured with all the weight training he had been doing, he could afford a few extra calories. Luke had definitely bulked up his wide shoulders and arms, and it made him feel good to be fit. Not to mention the glances he got from women, but Luke didn't pay any mind to that, he kept himself focused on the path ahead. If a girl was to be in the picture, then God would have to hit him on the head…after all at 33, he had plenty of time. He had to laugh at that thought because his mom totally disagreed!

The days flew and within thre weeks he had closed on his home and moved in. Luke was very pleased with his decision, and in no time he had the boxes unpacked and his stuff organized. He spent the next few days doing odd jobs around the home and especially enjoyed working in his yard. It was kind of fun discovering new plants and bushes that he had not really noticed…and it was during this 'discovery' time, when Luke bent over to examine a plant when a bucket of cold water hit him out of nowhere.

Luke howled, "For crying out loud, who did that?" He was drenched from head to toe, and looked over the fence to find the offender.

Hannah stiffened when she saw what she had done. She had no idea anyone was next door for it had been empty for several months. Looking down at the bucket, she knew she was doomed for the evidence was squarely in her hands. So she steeled herself for the confrontation and replied, "I'm am soooo very sorry sir, I truly did not see you."

Luke looked at the petite brunette with her hair tossed under a ball cap, blue jeans torn at the knees and a pink t-shirt that shouted 'Save the ta ta's.' Adorable? He thought. Absolutely. Guilty? Yes!

Hannah squirmed a bit until she realized he was going to be pleasant about her mishap.

Luke laughed as he held out his hand to shake hers. "I'm Luke Majors, your new neighbor."

Hannah peered from beneath her ball cap and observed she had dumped her bucket of water on a very handsome man, with the kindest eyes that matched his wide smile. Hannah extended her hand and replied, "Hi Luke, I'm Hannah Daniels." Luke eyed her again, this time he caught the color of her eyes…green, with gold flecks that completely dazzled him. "Oh great," he thought, "This was not in his plan."

Luke and Hannah talked for a few minutes, then he excused himself to put on dry clothes. Hannah also needed to leave, shedding her garden boots off at the door, she entered the laundry room off her back porch. She quickly pulled out her pink scrubs from the dryer, giving them a good shake before she showered for her next shift.

Hot water and steam were always a good combination to soothe her body and emotions. She grabbed her netted sponge and soaked it with honey-butter body wash, just the smell eased her soul. Trying to force her thoughts back to the hospital was a waste of time, they kept going straight to Luke's image, with his kind eyes and fabulous smile.

Just as she was getting out of the shower her pager beeped, looking at it she hurriedly dressed and dried her hair and threw on a little make-up...she had to deliver a baby and they never waited.

Luke tried to speculate on Hannah's life. She didn't wear a wedding ring, so possibly single. She drove a very nice SUV, top of the line, so that told him that whatever she did, it paid fairly well. He was definitely curious, but women were not in his plan right now...he figured if he said it enough he'd believe it!

After a very busy few days, Luke took his tour of the school in solitude, making mental notes where everything was located. Next, he worked on getting all his plans, projects and field trips lined up on paper. He prided himself in being thorough; he was ideal at crossing all the t's and dotting all the I's.

The first day of school arrived quickly and he was anticipating a great day. Luke jumped in his jeep, backing out very carefully as he always did...methodically. Hannah was coming home from her shift, a tad bleary eyed from birthing twins. Not paying close attention, she rammed into the back of Luke's jeep causing his head to jerk forward. Almost immediately, Hannah jumped into Doctor mode and ran to the driver's door where she leaned in and started to ask questions.

"Did you hit your head?"

"Does your neck hurt?"

"What about your back, does it feel alright?"

Luke looked a little dazed, but replied, "Are you a nurse?"

Hannah grinned, "No, a doctor, so be still and let me check you out." "And, by the way, I'm sorry about hitting your car."

"Yeah, I think I'm going to hide my dog…your track record so far isn't good." Luke grinned as she laughed.

They discussed getting his car fixed and then with a wave he was off, albeit a bit late for his first day of school, but at least on his way. Hannah stood there a few more moments tossing around those crazy feelings inside her head. She was already involved and Heath hinted he was ready to take it to the next level, but now she wasn't so sure. She needed some quiet time, so off to her back porch, grabbing her book, a glass of sweet tea and a pen just in case a word from God came. She wanted to make sure she wrote it down…!

As if Heath was reading her thoughts, he dropped in about an hour later. Before plopping himself into the rocker across from her, he gave her a quick kiss on the top of her head and smiled. "How was the birthing last night? You look exhausted."

"Do I look tired?" she retorted. "I thought I looked rather refreshed!" she said laughing at her sarcasm. "How was your work?" she asked. "The same as always, banking is never dull, but also not too exciting either… he said trailing off. Just constant and steady he laughed, like myself."

She smiled thinking he was so right, constant, steady, dependable, hardworking, loves God, but there just wasn't any passion or zing to the relationship. She needed bells to go off in her head, a little something… but there was nothing with Heath. He was everything you wanted in a guy…she just wasn't sure that he was hers.

At 32 years old, she had been given so much. God blessed her with brains, drive, a passion to help people, and good health. But, she was still single. The one thing she wanted so badly was to be a part of someone else's life…but, it had eluded her. Heath had been a contender, but now that she met Luke, well...

***

Luke had a great first day of high school. He was a good teacher, confident in his teaching methods and knew his purpose, and his passion was to teach kids. He was a kid at heart too, but he knew how to keep the balance of authority in check. Before long, the guys started coming by his house for a game of basketball or just to hang. Luke loved that...it was time well invested.

It wasn't long until Luke decided he needed a much bigger basketball area for the guys to play. He eyed his large back yard and imagined cementing a portion of it for his basketball court. He got estimates, consulted with experts and hired out the job. It was to be done while he was at school. He was not pleased about that, but it was on their time frame and not his. Friday rolled around and Luke anticipated a great day of coming home and the basketball area looking great. School went as usual, most of the kids did well on their history test, the Bible test not as much. Work to be done there. But, all in all a great day. On the way home, Luke was praying for God to open up a door to talk with his neighbor...she was a small powerhouse that drew him in. He tried to fight it, tried to deny it but it was there.

Luke's sporty SUV usually stopped at the mailbox but today he was anxious to see his yard. As he walked past the garage he heard a scream. Then he heard it again with garbled words. He ran to Hannah's gated fence when he stopped cold, blood draining from his face. He looked at Hannah, she looked back at him in disbelief as she slowly raised her arm pointing to the new basketball court that took up most of her backyard.

Luke practically staggered to the goal then slumped down on one of her adirondack chairs. "Oh No," he exclaimed. "How could this have happened?"

Hannah also in shock, was in despair over her lovely yard. Tears formed in her eyes and Luke groaned inwardly when he saw her eyes glisten over.

"Hannah, don't worry, they will have to fix this...it's their fault." He spoke in a soothing voice.

Hannah just laughed as the tears rolled...nothing more to say, nothing more she could do.

Luke staggered home an hour later. He was still stunned, and how this was going to be fixed was beyond him. Calls would be made first thing in the morning and then more calls to cancel the guy's game they had planned. He knew they would be greatly disappointed. The next morning, Luke took his cup of coffee out on his patio and started making calls when he heard Hannah call out to him over the fence.

"Can I join you for coffee?" she asked.

"Sure! Come on over!"

Hannah opened her gate and walked over grinning and said…

"I have this amazing basketball court in my backyard, do you want to come over and play?" Her eyes were dancing with mischief.

Luke grinned, "Are you any good," he said laughing.

"Well, after coffee you can see for yourself!"

Two hours later they were still talking, when he happened to mention that he'd better call the guys and cancel the game for tonight. He had also planned to cookout and make a big night of it, but it was not to be.

Hannah listened and before she thought about it she said, "Oh don't do that, y'all just come over and play and I'll help you cook the food. It would be fun and besides I love to cook."

Luke grinned and agreed on five o'clock to begin the christening of the basketball court.

Later, in the quiet of his home he looks up and says, "Really God, when I prayed for more time with Hannah I didn't mean for the cement to be poured in her yard! However, I know you got my back…so, I'll go with it."

He also had bad news to deliver. The contractor was booked until November, so that meant nothing could be done to her yard for two months. He dreaded telling her the news.

At four o'clock, Luke began hauling food over to Hannah's to get ready for the cookout and in the midst of splitting a soft drink, he shared the news. Hannah actually handled it just fine, no problem she said. She almost seemed happy about it.

They had a blast! The guys were great, Hannah was great with teenagers, cutting up and having fun. Luke also discovered what a great rapport they had between them. It was easy and he was confident that the pull between them was felt by both.

The evening was almost magical, even with the hot, sweaty teenagers they had amongst them. There was no denying the attraction, but now how was she to handle Heath. It wasn't fair to him if she was attracted to someone else. She needed to tell him, and with her doctor-like decision making skills, she phoned him for dinner.

"Hey Heath, how are you?"

"Great Hannah, and you?"

"Oh, I'm really good plus I have the night off, would you be interested in meeting for dinner at Henry's Restaurant in town?"

He agreed and the prayers began. The last thing she wanted to do was hurt Heath, but he needed to know that she was developing feelings for someone else.

They met at seven at Henry's. He spotted her and both followed the waiter, with Heath looking a bit sheepish, almost apologetic and she hadn't even said anything.

After ordering their food, Hannah began some small talk but something in her spirit told her something wasn't quite right with Heath. He was a little fidgety, maybe even distracted. Finally, she said something.

"Heath, is there something going on?" she inquired.

Heath looked a bit startled, then let out a small sigh. "Well, yes." He said.

Hannah just kept gazing on his face until he spoke again.

Heath looked sheepish again and then said, "I've met someone else and I feel we have a strong connection, but it kills me to think I may hurt you." He paused waiting for her reaction.

Hannah just set there for a second…stunned thinking, "How good was God? Only He could have orchestrated this!" Hannah grinned and reached for his hand, "It's all good Heath, because I have met someone else too…my neighbor!"

It was Heath's turn to look startled and then he laughed and raised his tea glass for a toast.

"Well, here is to good friends and future spouses!"

Hannah smiled.

***

Luke was back at home pondering. His mom always kidded him about his 'pondering and wandering' when he had issues of the heart. Luke would start pacing back and forth, then he'd walk the rooms, never realizing what he was doing as he was deep in thought. Today though, he was pondering his feelings for Hannah. He'd never felt this strongly for a woman… was this love? He thought so.

Relieved that he'd figured out his feelings, now came the hard part… what was he to do about them.

It was about that time that Hannah was doing the same thing. She had left Heath at the restaurant feeling good about their talk, and now she needed to think about her feelings for Luke. All she knew at the moment was how her heart skipped a beat when she saw him, and how kind and loving he was…even with the basketball court mix-up, he never got angry or overly upset, he just took it in stride. She liked that. Her mom always said how a man handles himself in tense situations says a lot about his character.

Hannah was about to arrive home when her phone rang, it was Luke.

"Hey, you want to have some coffee before you turn in for the night?" he asked.

"Why sure, I'd love to…do you want me to come over?"

But before he could answer, she pulled in her driveway and saw him at the gate…smiling.

"What are you up to Luke?" she asked as she stepped out of her SUV.

He just smiled and guided her to the back yard. It was beautiful! Luke had strung up white lights in her oak trees, mason jars hung from some of the branches with tea lights flickering, and there was a small patio set placed on the basketball goal area with coffee and dessert arranged artfully. There was even soft music playing in the background.

"How did you manage this?" she asked in pure surprise.

He just winked at her and said, "I called in the troops from school and they loved hanging like monkeys from the branches stringing lights up. I somehow managed the rest."

Hannah stepped a little closer to Luke and asked, "Why did you do all this?"

Luke's eyes locked with hers and said, "Because…I'm falling for the girl-next-door."

Hannah felt her heart skip as she said, "Fall away, I'll catch you," as he leaned down and kissed her.

She could have sworn she heard bells…

"Perhaps this is the moment for which you were created."
Ester 4:14

The Christmas Ring

Kicking the tire with her new boots then stomping the ground like a two year old, Lily fussed and fumed over her flat-tire. She was absolutely beside herself as she grabbed her cell phone and walked around with her hand up in the air trying desperately to get a signal.

"Lord, pleaseeeee let me get a signal, and I promise I will make time to do the next Bible study the church offers."

No signal.

"God…really, please I'm on a dirt road, in the middle of nowhere and it's getting cold."

"HELLO…God do you hear me?!" Lily shouted out.

Still no signal. Still no answer. Still getting cold and dark.

Lily sat in her SUV despairing over the fact that she never watched her dad change a tire. Then scolding herself for going on this wild goose chase so late in the day. But, the lead was entirely too tempting, and having the opportunity to buy some really neat primitive cupboards for the store was just too much for Lily to pass up.

Lily smiled as she thought about her store, "So Prim" and how successful God had allowed it to become. The location was in an old log cabin she was able to purchase at the end of Main Street in town. It was the perfect backdrop for her antiques and displays. From fall to spring was her favorite time of year to decorate. But, it was close to the end of October, so that meant she needed to gear up for the Thanksgiving and

Christmas open house.

That afternoon, when she got the new lead for primitives, Lily headed to the bank to grab cash for purchases such as these and headed north with her GPS plugged in. Looking back now, it wasn't the best decision since she was alone in the backwoods, and still not quite sure how far from the house she was.

Lily looked in the back seat and grabbed her quilt she had stashed in for emergencies and wrapped herself in it. Sitting there was driving her crazy so she promptly made the decision to walk. Lugging the quilt around her shoulders, she grabbed her purse and locked up her car.

"I cannot believe I am in this situation." Lily grumbled.

"Ouch!" she grabbed a nearby tree as she stumbled over the above ground roots.

"For Heaven's Sake," she ranted to the tree, "Don't you know your roots are supposed to grow underground?"

On and on she whined then pleaded with God, who she felt was NOT listening nor did He care about her at the moment. Then a thought occurred to her, maybe God doesn't speak "whinese," Lily giggled at the mere thought of that.

"Okay God, I need some light to see, it's getting a little dark and eerie."

About that same moment, a truck comes down the hill with lights blaring.

Lily waved and the truck stopped and a man's head popped out the window.

"Hey Miss, do you need some help?"

Oh, my goodness, now why would a man ask that when a woman is on a dirt road, in the woods and it's dark…ugh! She thought.

But instead she said, "Yes, my car has a flat tire…can you fix it?"

"Not tonight…no light." He said.

"Well, can you take me home?" she said.

"No can't take you home, I can't get around your car, unless I cut down some trees and I'm not going to do that." He grinned.

Moaning, Lily thought, "What am I going to do?" Then decided to ask,

"You wouldn't happen to know Eli Stanford would you?"

"That would be me," Eli said.

"You?" Lily looked puzzled.

"That's right," he said.

"But, I thought you would be much older, you see, I was told you had some primitive cupboards you might be interested in selling?"

Eli leaned back in his Ford F250 truck and eyed Lily for a split moment. Guessing late twenties, early thirties, shoulder length hair and in the dimmed light from the truck it looked more reddish than brown. Definitely a pretty woman and a tad spirited he figured with the red in her hair.

"Well, not sure how much older you were expecting, but I'm thirty-five and I do have several cupboards and such to sell to the right person. These pieces are generational in the Stanford family so they need someone who understands their value in price and historical value."

Lily shivered suddenly from the cold, and Eli jumped out of the truck and insisted that she go back to the house with him. Lily was too tired and cold to protest, and hoped she was making the correct judgment that he was a good decent man.

Eli spoke quietly, "My sister, Ellen is at the house, she's staying for a few more months until she gets her Masters in Christian Education, then she's hoping to go into missions somewhere.

Lily eased up a bit then, with a Christian sister around, he couldn't be too bad.

They talked easily for the few minutes it took to get to his house, she explained her primitive antique business and he spoke of his passion for teaching history to high school students in town.

With surprise in her voice Lily said, "Why haven't I ever met you? I thought I knew just about everyone around."

"Well, we've only been here for two months; I just accepted the offer to replace the history teacher going out on maternity leave and won't be coming back." Eli stopped the truck and looked at her with a grin, "so now you know everybody there is to know in town that is."

Lily ignored the little jab and got out of the truck. For some unknown reason, he got under her skin just enough to intrigue and irritate.

Hesitating for a second as Eli opened the door to his quaint farmhouse, Lily entered with pure amazement as she looked around the family room, so beautifully decorated in farmhouse/primitive style it could have been in any country magazine.

"Did you do this Eli?" she asked in amazement.

"Well, my sister is the decorator, although I do have my opinions."

Lily walked around, touching the old wood with remnants of milk paint on them. Yellow ware covered the top of one cupboard, wooden bowls filled with all sorts of interesting items and the reproduction of lighting took you absolutely back in time. All the while Lily was looking, Eli built a fire and pulled a rocker closer to it as he motioned for her to sit and get warm.

Lily looked at Eli's profile as he stoked the fire. Black stubble with a touch of gray covered his face, framing his great smile. Not quite sure of his eyes, but they were kind, that she was sure of.

Eli stood and walked towards a wide reddish brown cupboard stacked with quilts and grabbed a couple tossing them on the sofa.

"I'll take the sofa and you can have my room," he said smiling thankful he'd put clean sheets on his bed earlier that morning.

"Oh no, I cannot take your room Eli," but her refusal was ignored and he ushered her into his room. Saying goodnight she crawled into the bed, kicking her boots off as she climbed in. Too tired to look around she fell asleep

Waking up to the smell of coffee, Lily jumped out of bed in a panic. Gathering her thoughts she remembered the events of last night and calmed down. She glanced at herself in the mirror above his chest of drawers and gasped.

"Oh my, she muttered, I need a rubber band or a hat. Looking around she found both, although the sports hat was not her team. Lily pulled her short pony tail through the back of the hat, washed her face and even brushed her teeth with the spare toothbrush she happened to have in her purse from a recent cleaning.

Whew, Lily thought, not my best, but at least not scary.

She walked around the corner following the aroma of the coffee and found Eli perched on a stool looking at his laptop.

"Good morning Eli," she said brightly.

"Well good morning to you, Lily," he said noting his hat she was wearing, and said, "Nice hat you're wearing."

"Oh, I hope you don't mind, but my hair was a bit scary."

"I hardly think it was scary...but, the hat's a nice touch," he said grinning.

Eli placed a cup of coffee in front of her and they chatted like old friends.

After they ate bagels, Eli offered to show her the cupboards he was willing to part with in the back room.

Eli pointed to the three step back cupboards, and Lily sucked in her breath at the fabulous shape they were in.

"They are in such wonderful condition, I am stunned by their quality," Lily said.

Eli walked over to the first one, and spoke of their history.

"You know these began in the Stanford family several generations ago. It started with my great, great, great, grandfather who began his home in the mid 1800s. His name was also Eli Stanford and his wife was Ellen. I've been told they were a special couple, and my sister and I were named after them. If these cupboards could talk, they would tell you about the Christmas ring."

"Christmas ring?" Lily repeated, quite curious.

"Yes, there was a glorious ruby ring passed down through the generations. The oldest Stanford son would give the ring to the one he chose to marry on Christmas morning. It was said this ring represented Christ's love for us, the gold filigree stood for Jesus' birth, the ruby was for the blood He shed, and the circle was for His eternal promise. The Christmas ring was a Stanford promise that she would always be his forever girl."

Lily's eyes filled with tears, she was so moved she couldn't speak. After a couple of moments and at least one good swallow, Lily asked the obvious question, "Who is wearing the ring now?"

Eli looked at Lily and replied, "The Christmas ring was lost when my mother died suddenly and the ring was not on her finger. My mother had the habit of taking it off at night and hiding it in different places. She was always afraid something might happen to it. We searched every nook and cranny, but to no avail, no one has even been able to find the Christmas ring."

"What an inspiring story Eli, such a Godly, romantic family heritage you have."

Eli laughed out loud, "So now you see why I'm not married at thirty-five, I don't have the ring to carry on the family's romantic heritage."

Lily laughed at Eli's confession and also how he was quickly changing the subject.

"So, how about these cupboards? Are you willing to negotiate a price Lily?"

Lily grinned, "You can count on it," she said with a wink.

The number came to quite a high number, but they were worth it. Lily hoped to make a nice profit and someone would be getting a fabulous piece to display in their home. She just wished it could be her home it was so tempting to keep one, but she needed to keep the store going.

One week later Lily had the cupboards moved in her store, thanks to Eli's muscles and good nature. She was also secretly thrilled at his positive reaction, for some reason his approval meant a lot to her.

Lily worked hard to get the store ready for the Christmas Open

House scheduled the weekend before Thanksgiving. Every night she would stay several hours after closing, decorating with candles, white twinkle lights intertwined in grapevine, nativities were tucked in special spots and the scent of Christmas was everywhere. During this time, Eli was a frequent drop-in, coming by after school. A couple of times, he brought dinner, saving her from starvation as they ate amongst the unopened boxes of merchandise.

The evening before open house, Lily was fooling with the step-back cupboard that had the beautiful patina along with touches of green milk paint in just the right places. It was her favorite and her heart tugged every time she touched it knowing she had the perfect spot for it in her home. She bent down and opened the bottom doors to hide merchandise until needed when her hand bumped a protruding knot in the wood on the right side close to the door.

Lily jumped up to get the hammer to tap it back in place when Eli knocked on the door. Opening the door, he handed her a cup of coffee and her favorite pumpkin donut.

"Thought you might need a bit of caffeine and sugar to get you through the evening," Eli said,

"You have saved me!" Lily practically squealed. "You have no idea how much I need this jolt to keep me going. In fact, I was just hunting my hammer, which, who knows where it is in this chaos."

"What did you need the hammer for Lily," Eli asked.

"Well, when I was putting extra merchandise in the green cupboard for hiding, my hand hit a knot in the wood that was protruding, so I thought I would tap it back in place."

Finally Lily spotted the hammer right where she had left it, on the ladder she was using to hang lights."

"Here, let me do that for you," Eli said. "Now where did you say it was exactly?"

"On the right side after you open the door," she replied.

Oh I see, he thought, but after looking at it, for some reason it just seemed odd to protrude like that. With that thought, Eli took the other side of the hammer and gently pulled the knot out which strangely did not affect the outside of the cupboard. The knot popped out and taped on the other side was a ring a ruby red ring.

Eli, who was squatting at the time trying to pry the knot off, fell back abruptly in amazement.

"Lily," he yelled, "come here." Lily dropped her handful of snow-men and ran towards Eli.

"What's the matter?"

"Look what popped out of the cupboard, Lily...It's the Christmas ring, the family ring!"

Eli was so excited he was beside himself.

Lily took the ring from his hand and her eyes grew big. "This ring is absolutely gorgeous Eli," she said almost in a reverent whisper.

Eli was still stunned, then he became overwhelmed that it had been almost lost forever. But Lily, whose love for the old, and was curious about every inch of every piece, had saved the ring.

Eli walked up to Lily and grabbed her face gently with his hands, kissed her forehead saying thank you. Lily held her breath, wanting more, couldn't he see it? Did he feel anything for her?

Eli put the ring in his jean pocket then hugged her knowing that if he kissed her again, she would know how he felt and he wasn't quite sure he was ready.

The Open House was a huge success. Lily's creative touches were amazing and drew in a huge crowd. Apple cider and toffee shortbread were consumed in large quantities, and Christmas music put the cus-tomers in a sweet, happy buying mood. If you could have a perfect Open House, this was it and her favorite part was Eli was right along-side her charming the customers.

Eli was a bit tired after a week of teaching and a long night of help-ing Lily at the store. He crawled into bed and pondered all night about how he felt about her, and without a doubt he knew his life would never be quite complete without her.

Eli took Lily out several times, dining in restaurants, walks in the mountains, driving to estate sales looking for that perfect bargain for the store. Eli even cooked for her one night, it was the night Lily knew without any doubts that he was the one for her. But, did he feel the same?

Christmas morning came and Lily had arrived early to spend Christmas morning with Eli and then they would be off to have Christmas dinner with her folks. In the family room, Eli had a roaring fire for her and presents under the tree.

Lily sat in the rocker near the fire, her favorite place to sit. Eli stood nearby watching her look so content. Her hair shimmered in the firelight, and her face glowed. He walked over and knelt beside her and asked her to be his wife, his "forever girl." He brought the Christmas ring out of his pocket and placed it on her finger. The ring was home, on the hand it belonged.

Lily's eyes filled with tears…as she looked at the ring knowing the Godly heritage it carried.

Eli pulled her up close to him whispering in her ear, "I have one more surprise for you."

Lily couldn't even imagine what that could be, so she just walked beside him to the dining room and followed his gaze to the beloved green cupboard that had held the Christmas ring, wrapped with a big red bow. She gasped with pleasure.

"Merry Christmas, Lily" he murmured as he gathered her once more into his arms.

Her heart was full…

"Come to me all who are weary and I will give you rest."
Matthew 11:28

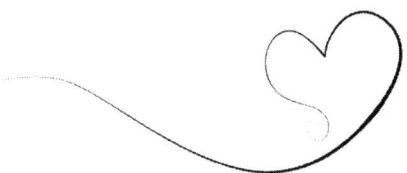

A Wink And A Promise

*L*ove was in the air...it always was in the spring, especially in 1953. I was walking home with my sister, Joyce and our friend Bernice. I would be lying if I said we weren't a bit flirty back then, the spring just brings it out in young people. Slowly walking home from school this particular day, I could even feel my hips swaying just a bit more exaggerated almost in cadence with the trees limbs stirring. Lost in my thoughts, I didn't hear a car approaching until a quick blast of the horn jolted me.

Honk...honk, "Hey ladies, need a ride home?" asked a very handsome sailor decked out in uniform. Dark, thick, wavy hair peeked out from his cap; very tan almost glossy skin framed his smoky gray eyes and startling white teeth. The uniform, oh my, dare I remember the white uniform; I was so captivated by his good looks it almost overtook me.

"Well, ladies," he persisted.

Bernice looked closer at his face and said, "Leonard...is that you? Why, I haven't seen you in ages!" she gushed. I didn't know why she was gushing because she already had a boyfriend, I think he just had that effect.

Leonard smiled and my heart danced...I wondered if he could see my heart doing the twist?

"I've been in the Navy for a year, Bernice and I've missed seeing everyone...so can I give you ladies a life?"

"Sure," said Bernice as she plopped herself in the front seat. Joyce and I retreated to the back. I sat directly behind Leonard just knowing he could see me breathing funny...or was I breathing? Looking back, I don't think I was.

As he put the car in gear and steered back onto the road, Leonard looked up into the rear-view mirror and winked at me while giving me a devilish grin. That was it! I was his...forever and ever, Amen. Before, he could get us home, I had already planned our wedding, our children and our growing old years. It was his fault, he shouldn't have winked, but he did. Later, he told me I was his 'pick-up' girl. I secretly etched that into my heart.

We married the summer of '54. It was a hot steamy day. We took our vows for "better or worse" "richer or poorer" and "sickness and health till death do us part", in the Methodist Church. My mom said it would never last because his kinfolk were from the other side of the tracks. But, in my mind, there is always a pearl amongst the grit and he was my pearl.

The marriage went well and within a few years so did the children. We had two girls, one I named after a soap opera star...Lisa-Rae and when my second daughter was born on Halloween, we named her Lori-Gaye with an "i," I think we set a trend, plus I like names that rhyme— it's the writer in me.

I had planned on us being richer than we were, but comfortable is what happened. We're just fine. Everything's paid for...we're grateful to God for that especially since I had a stroke.

Yes, our growing old years were the only ones that didn't go as we hoped for. We had just booked a Hawaiian cruise with all the bells and whistles; our dream-come-true trip that we had wanted to take for years.

Couldn't go; doctors said no.

I'm paralyzed on the left side of my body. Everything works except for my arm which quietly stays by my side, and my leg is braced, but I can walk slowly with a cane.

I'm grateful, but...

There are always "buts" in life. God doesn't want "buts" he wants "praise and gratefulness" because he knows what's best for our life... even if He chooses not to heal my stroke.

So, after 55 years of marriage, three daughters (one snuck in much later, Kristi-Kay with an "I") and eight grandchildren, we proved mother wrong.

He's still my pearl that I clasped around my heart in '53.

Every now and then he'll tell me I'll always be his 'pick-up' girl as he picks me up from a chair or the bed or he tries to lift my spirits on a bad day.

Those words are forever etched into my heart...for better or worse, in sickness and in health, I'll always be his 'pick-up' girl and he'll always be my sailor-boy.

"Guard your heart above all else, for it determines
the course of your life." Proverbs 4:23

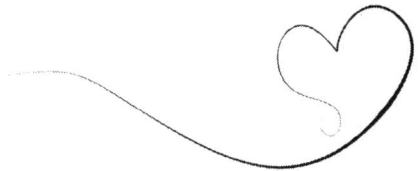

Fires Of The Heart

The cabin was small, hidden partially under large oaks keeping the sun at bay. Light escaped through the cracks in the chinking casting shadows on the rough plank flooring. The fire had died down and needed stoking before it totally went out leaving a definite chill in the air. Eli stared at the dying embers knowing he needed to get up and tend to it but just couldn't make his legs move. Instead, he ran his calloused hands through his dark hair and groaned. His voice was deep and guttural, a painful cry that shattered his heart. Essie, his bride of one year had died of the fever. Just a week ago, they celebrated their one year anniversary with a special dinner she cooked up and a night cuddled together by the fire. Now she was gone.

The grave was fresh...with wilted daisies still scattered on the top with a very rough cross he had made place at the head. He had inscribed with a knife, "Beloved Wife, Essie Rose Stanford 1880-1902. Tears rolled down his face as he recalled the moment then he willed himself to place wood on the fire and stoke it.

It was that moment, that very moment that a drop of anger entered in. Eli felt its entrance but his heart was too weak to fight. The festering began to take place and before long it not only controlled but fueled his life.

Eli stopped going to church in town, he quit being neighborly and polite. He pushed his and Essie's Bible under the bed as not to be seen nor reminded of God's goodness and provision. No reminder was needed, God took it all away.

He worked hard on the farm, working from sun up to sun down. He didn't rest often because if he did, he would think of Essie, feel the grief and he didn't want to feel, he just wanted to keep moving.

But, his best bud Jeremy wouldn't leave him alone. Every few days, he'd wander over on his horse and see about him.

"Eli," Jeremy called out, "I see you need some help with the weeding of the garden."

"No, I'm good," Eli barked back.

"Doesn't look good, Eli," Jeremy said grinning.

"Why don't you just head back to your family and leave me alone. I am fine." Eli exploded.

"Wish I could do that my friend, but the Lord won't let me..." and with that Jeremy turned his horse around and headed back home. But not before yelling, "I'll be back Eli."

Eli had to grin at his friend's persistence...hardheaded he was, but a true friend.

Dropping his hoe to the ground, Eli slumped against Essie's favorite oak tree. He was plum bone weary, at twenty-nine he had worked his body beyond it's limit. Breathing heavily, he looked up at the heaven's and shook his fist at God.

"Why did you have to take her from me? She was my wife, the one you chose to stand by me, where is she now? Why did you need her?"

Letting out a sob that had been held back for so long, he released his pain, spilling tears on the soil. It felt good to cry.

Two weeks later Eli was short on supplies, salt, flour, sugar along with other staples that he needed. He hooked up his wagon to his horse and clicked the reins.

The air felt invigorating. Essie loved autumn, it had been her favorite time of the year. She loved making pumpkin pies as much as she loved eating them. He inhaled the air again almost swearing he could smell the cinnamon spice.

Eli rounded the curve on the dirt road into town and braked his wagon next to the General Store. Taking out his list, he handed it to the store manager to gather it together. Eli waited out front when Essie's good friend, Lily bumped into him.

"Oh, excuse me Eli," Lily said in an apologetic voice.

"I had so much in my hands, I wasn't paying attention to where I was going."

"No harm Lily, how are you doing?"

"Good, really good. I guess you heard I'm getting married next week?"

"No, I didn't know," Eli smiled as he continued on, "who's the lucky fella."

"It's Jeremy's younger brother, Joshua. You remember Josh don't you."

"Of course Lily, I'm happy for you."

"Thanks Eli, and how have you been since...since Essie's death, Eli?"

Eli felt himself tense up. How did she think he'd been doing? But, instead he answered, "Fine, Lily, just fine."

Thankfully, his order was ready and he excused himself to load up the wagon and head back home to his safe sanctuary...alone.

Winter came and went. Eli kept the fireplace going non-stop and lived basically off of dried meats and hard bread that he tried to make like Essie's but to no avail. Jeremy came a few times and always brought baked goods from his wife and they were indeed appreciated. It was taking time, but he felt the anger and bitterness start to wane. He still mourned for Essie but the nights were becoming more bearable.

Spring was approaching again, and the town folk were ready for a picnic party along the riverbank. Word of mouth spread the details for the Sunday afternoon picnic and Eli decided to join in. Being a widower, he was exempt from bringing food, however, he did bring a few apples for good measure.

Eli spruced up a bit, not that he had to do too much to his already handsome rugged face. A bath, a shave and a clean shirt did him a world of good. He was meticulous about his straight white teeth, a rarity seen around town. Eli showed up on time and loaded his plate with the fried chicken and potatoes and as many of the slices of cake and pie his plate would hold. He teetered just a bit on his feet as he tried to balance his plate without spilling when he bumped into a young woman. Food flew everywhere causing a commotion.

"Oh, sorry, so sorry," Eli exclaimed.

Annie looked up at Eli then back at her hair, her just washed and curled hair had globs of sweet apple pie filling stuck in the strands. Her eyes were big and horrified!

"My hair is a mess," she cried out in frustration.

Eli walked closer and said, "Hang on just a minute and I'll try to get it out." He grabbed a cloth and quickly ran to the river to wet it, then slowly wiped her hair clean.

"Good as new," he said smiling.

"Not quite, but better," Annie laughed a bit now.

"By the way, I'm Eli Stanford," he said.

"I'm Annie Anderson," she said as she extended her hand to his.

"Are you here alone Annie or with family?"

"I'm with my mom and dad for a while, until I can get settled in town. I am the new school teacher for the children."

Eli looked at Annie in amazement. "Why you don't look old enough to be a school teacher."

Annie's back prickled up and replied, "Well, just because I'm short and little doesn't mean I'm not old enough...I'm twenty-five and very capable!"

Eli laughed and said, "Whoa there! I didn't mean to insult you...I was actually paying you a compliment. Being young looking is a good thing."

Annie paused a moment before responding, "I'm sorry, just a little sensitive as I seem to always have to prove my age and my authority at school."

Eli thought it was a bit odd that a woman as pretty as Annie wasn't married or have a beau. At least, he didn't see one nearby to keep the other men away. In the midst of his thoughts, Eli began to twist his wedding ring that was still on his left hand. Annie noticed and drew in her breath, "Oh no," she thought, "He's married."

Annie looked up at Eli and politely excused herself from the situation. He was the first man that made her heart skip since Henry died in a horse accident two years ago, and of course, he had to be married!

Eli watched Annie walk off wondering what he'd said. He hated to say it but Essie was right, he was totally clueless when it came to women. She always would fuss when he couldn't figure out what was on her mind. He would beg her to tell him, but all she would say was, "you should already know." His answer was always the same... "How can I know if you don't tell me?"

But, Annie pricked his interest. Yes, she was pretty, any old fool could see that. A tiny figure loaded with spirit to match her reddish blonde hair. Her face was fair with just a few freckles sprinkled across her nose. Dazzling green eyes framed with long black eyelashes. Yes, she was definitely a catch but what was her story?

A little later Eli caught a glimpse of Annie with her parents he supposed. They were grouped together eating ice cream when he noticed a little girl sitting in her lap. He couldn't tell, but she seemed around the ago of four. Was this her daughter?

- - -

Annie talked with her mom and dad a bit as her daughter squirmed in her lap.

"Mommy, can I get down now and play with the others?" she asked ever so sweetly.

Annie looked down into her daughter's mischievous eyes and said, "You may as long as you stay where I can see you."

Sarah grinned, "I will mommy," and off she went.

Annie sighed to herself as she watched her lovely daughter play. Henry had been so proud of her, and he loved showing her off. She missed him and how sad she was for Sarah who would barely remember her daddy.

Her eyes grew misty, so she excused herself from her parents and walked to the river but was still where she could keep an eye on Sarah. She dabbed her eyes with her handkerchief and stuffed it back into the skirt pocket. She had so much to prepare for now, a new home, a new job and continuing to raise Sarah alone. She could only think of it in bits and pieces, if she thought of it in its entirety, she felt faint.

Sensing she was not alone, she turned around and there was Eli.

"Oh Eli, I did not hear you come over." She said.

"I saw you standing alone and you seemed sad, so I thought I'd make sure you were alright."

Annie smiled, "Thank you Eli, I'm fine...really, I'm just a bit overwhelmed with my new life, or rather Sarah's and my new life."

"Sarah?" he inquired.

"Sarah's my daughter, she is almost four years old. Her daddy died two years ago and I'm just getting on my feet and trying to do what is best for both of us."

Eli nodded his understanding. "I know how you feel Annie, I lost my wife Essie, a year ago and it's been difficult to go on, but you do."

Annie's eyes pooled again in sadness for her new friend. "I am sorry Eli, I do understand; is there anything I can do to help?"

Eli grinned, "Thanks Annie, just talking to you helps." Eli tipped his hat and walked off.

He was a bit lighter in step learning she was alone, maybe...just maybe he could get to know her better.

Annie too was lighter in step, she was definitely attracted to him but she had to be careful. It wasn't just about her, she had Sarah to protect.

Gathering her remaining food and saying goodbye to her parents, she called out to Sarah to come on, they needed to get back home and get ready for tomorrow's first day of school.

- - -

Monday morning came early and after walking Sarah to her parent's house for a few hours, she headed north on the main street that went through town. It wasn't too far, just at the edge of town and she needed to be early to get the classroom ready.

She was certainly surprised when she entered the one room class that Eli was there starting the stove for her. He had even carried wood from outside and placed it in the wood box near the stove.

"Oh my, I didn't expect to see you this morning Eli." She said with a bit too much pleasure.

Eli ever so slightly blushed and pushed his hat back allowing some of his dark hair to fall casually on his forehead.

"Well, I just thought I'd help the teacher a but since this was your first day and all."

Annie thanked him and walked him to the door. "I so appreciate your kindness Eli; how can I thank you?"

"I'll come up with something later," he replied with a wink and walked out.

Annie giggled...she didn't know she still could.

From then on Eli showed up first thing and lit the stove and got it going for her. He would say, "you need to teach the kids, not worry about the store or if the children were cold."

Annie got so used to seeing him every morning it totally changed her routine. She definitely primped a bit more, and made sure her clothes were in good order. So, when she walked in this morning and Eli wasn't there and the stove wasn't going she became worried.

So much that she canceled school after two hours of teaching to the delight of the children. She walked home rather quickly, hitched up the wagon and rode to Eli's home. It was quite a charming location with huge trees hovering near the log home. The porch was large and clean with two rockers beside each other. Smoke was coming out of the chimney but, nowhere was Eli.

Annie tied up the horse, and walked up the two porch steps to the front door and banged loudly. No response. She opened the door to an empty home. Confused, she ran to the barn calling out his name. "Eli, it's me Annie," she cried out. She stood still hoping to hear any sounds, but none came. She noticed his horse was gone. "Where could he be," she thought.

Annie unhitched her horse and rode bareback toward the garden where she saw him stooped over weeding.

"What are you doing Eli?" She yelled as she slid off her horse.

"Weeding?" he said startled.

"You scared me to death Eli," she cried.

Eli ran over to her and grabbed her shoulders, "I'm fine Annie, I overslept and knew I wouldn't make it, so I just got an early start here instead. I'm sorry for scaring you. So, why were you scared Annie?" he said with a twinkle in his eye.

Tears still pouring out of Annie's eyes just made her mad as she jerked out of his clasp.

"I don't know, I was just used to seeing you every morning and then when you weren't there today, I was scared you were hurt."

Eli sucked in his breath. It never occurred to him that she would be concerned. I guess that's why Essie always said he was clueless.

"Oh Annie, I'm really sorry."

"Well since you're fine, I'm leaving." She said rather snappy.

Eli ran after her and pulled her into his arms. "Annie don't go...stay."

"Why?" she asked.

Eli's mouth grew dry, he had not said the word love since Essie died. "Because I love you." He said as he leaned in and kissed her.

Annie melted as she put her arms around his neck and returned the kiss before sliding out of his arms and looking up at him.

"What do we do now?" she asked.

Eli looked down on his petite fireball and grinned, "Well, first we're going to your parents so I can talk with your father, and pick up Sarah, then we'll come back here and I'll cook up some dinner for you both."

Annie was not used to being told what to do, and started to protest, but Eli gave her a look that stopped her words.

"Annie," he said, "I love you both, and I need to explain this to your father first."

Annie looked up at Eli and said, "No, first I want to see Essie's grave."

Eli was taken by surprise, "Why?" he asked.

"Because Essie was your first love, I want to know her, I need you to tell me about her. Are we alike? Totally different?" Annie asked.

Eli led her back to the rocking chairs on the front porch seating her in Essie's. He leaned back in his and closed his eyes as he talked.

"Essie was an amazing woman. She was kind, compassionate, understanding and foremost a deeply spiritual woman. She loved children, but she died before we could have any. She made me laugh. I never felt I was good enough for her but she loved me in spite of my weaknesses."

Annie smiled and said, "I wish I could have known her, I think we'd been friends."

Eli replied, "Y'all would have been."

"How about Henry, what was he like?" Eli asked.

Annie's mind wandered to the five years they had been married. "He was a wonderful husband and father, Eli. He worked hard for us, providing a nice home and didn't fuss when I needed him to build me a cabinet for the china my grandmother gave me. He said, 'Don't know what we're going to do with china in the west, but if you want to have a tea party with Sarah, then I'll build you a china cabinet.' Annie laughed, we still have it in my home. It's a treasure for Sarah to keep one day. He put up with all my foolishness and would say, he was the luckiest man in the world. But, I was the lucky one."

Eli looked over at Annie and grabbed her hand, "I think the best way to honor Essie's and Henry's love is to love again, right Annie?" He asked as he kissed her hand.

Annie nodded as she thanked God for giving her two wonderful men to love in her life.

- - -

A few weeks later, under the oak tree next to the house, Annie and Eli exchanged vows to love and honor each other. Henry and Essie were there in spirit as they committed their lives to God, their marriage and to Sarah. They even brought out the china to serve the punch afterwards. They didn't have a long honeymoon since school was still in session, but Eli said that was okay...he knew how to keep the fires going.

Indeed.

"For I know the plans I have for you declares the Lord.
Plans to prosper you and not to harm you, plans to give you a
hope and a future." Jeremiah 29:11

Captivated

"Mom," Elisabeth called out, "where is my pink sundress?" Lori dropped the towels on the laundry room floor and walked down the hall.

"Elisabeth, you are such a slob honey! If you would pick up those piles of clothes on the floor you just might find your pink dress." Grinning, Lori turned muttering to herself, "She did not get that trait from me...it was definitely her father's."

Elisabeth grinned back. She knew she was a little bit of a clutter bug so she dug a little deeper in the pile and sure enough, there was the pink sundress.

"Mom," she yelled out again, "would you have time to iron it while I take a shower?"

"Honestly, I am going to change my name from Mom to maid... at least the title would fit me better!" Lori grabbed the dress as Elisabeth gave her a hug saying, "Thanks mom."

"Well, I hope John is worth all of this effort."

Lori spoke with a smile, "He is Mom. I just feel that only once in a blue moon you meet a guy like this."

"Like what, honey?"

"Well, John has such a Godly character with a strength that amazes me, and under his sweet, gentle spirit he has a very protective nature."

Lori put the iron down and stared at the dress. At that moment, her motherly instinct kicked in and she knew...he was the one.

After her shower, Elisabeth flitted around in excitement combing her honey-blonde hair then slipping into her dress where she was really 'no bigger that a minute' as the southerners would say. Elisabeth was, without a doubt, the little sister of the family protected by her two older and much bigger brothers. Definitely, between John and the brothers, she was well looked after. She was also a woman of strength, and she continuously kept her pink Bible in her purse. Elisabeth had a way of attracting people with her naturally quiet spirit exuding who she was in Christ.

Months clicked by quickly and the words 'I love you' became the daily ending on the phone each night. Elisabeth was deeply in love for the first time and she felt that God had given her favor with such a man as John.

* * *

John absolutely loved her in pink. Early before the sun rose, she dressed in her bathing suit and pulled the pink sundress over it. Walking down to the beach gave her a renewed spirit as she gazed at the vastness of the ocean. Sitting on the sand still warm from the sun the day before, Elisabeth drew a double heart in the sand...connecting hearts, one still beating and one lay still in the sand. Tears rolled down her cheeks as she choked back emotions of grief. The rawness she felt swept memories in and out of her mind. John's battle with cancer humbled her. Elisabeth knew the first night they met that he had a rare, non-curable cancer. But, they were fiercely drawn together, neither could pull away nor did they want to.

In the beginning of their relationship the cancer stayed at his heels like a hungry dog. They enjoyed dates, the lake, friends and other stuff. But, it crept in a little more each day...relentless, like a stalker. The pain was intense, the treatment difficult and the outcome poor. But, Elisabeth never wavered her faith for she knew God had brought them together... not to break apart.

The tumors were ruthless as they ravaged his body, and the prayers were screamed into the night from Elisabeth, "Lord...please, heal him."

But, the healing did not come.

John's writings were like those of a modern day prophet...tilling journal after journal. He wrote notes to Elisabeth, encouraging her with his love but knowing he had to let her go. His earthly misson complete, the Kingdom awaited his arrival.

Elisabeth grabbed her beach bag and pulled out the last unread note John was able to scribble with his deteriorated body. Her hands felt numb as she opened the envelope. Glancing towards the ocean for a breath of salty air, Elisabeth read his final words to her.

Elisabeth...only once in a blue moon do you find a love like ours. Truly, the King and I are captivated by your beauty. Live your life with love and purpose knowing that is what you gave me. I love you...John.

"Oh John, it was I who was captivated by your beauty," Elisabeth whispered.

Laying her head on the two hearts in the sand...she wept.

"In the morning, O Lord, you hear my voice; In the morning
I lay my requests before you and wait in expectation."
Psalm 5:3

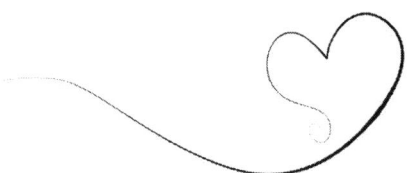

Moms Just Know

Digging through the boxes Marci found the large red hat box that her mama loved. Red was her color and large hats her signature. She was southern classy, and a little bit sassy. Just pulling out the hat and trying it on made her giggle as she walked to the mirror to catch her reflection. Marci had the perfect oval face to frame her mass of blonde hair that she controlled with a side pony-tail. For fun, Marci cut her dark syrupy eyes over at the mirror catching her reflection and smiled. Just thinking of her mother tugged at her heart. Yesterday had been a tough day at the Infusion Center where she received her next to last treatment. All the nurses loved Sylvia's bodacious personality and losing her hair just gave her an excuse to buy more hats. But, this red hat was special, it was her celebratory sign for the last chemo session next week. No doubt her mom would enter and exit the center in true Southern sass…by sporting her red hat.

Placing the hat back into the box, Marci tidied up the room and went to check on her mom. Sylvia was sitting up in her recliner, Bible in her lap, a hot cup of tea that was more for keeping her hands warm than for sipping.

"Hey darling," Sylvia smiled hoping the lightness in her speech covered up the discomfort.

"Hi mom," Marci smiled back but sensed rather than saw her mother's pain.

"How about a pillow behind your back?" Marci inquired as she grabbed the one on the sofa and stuffed it behind her.

Sylvia smiled saying, "can't hide anything from you can I?

Marci laughed, "No mom and you could never hide it from Dad either."

"No, no I couldn't, he knew me so well. I miss him every day," her mother whispered while tears sprang into her eyes. Marci sat and held her hand until the moment passed. This was just so hard, and absolutely no manual to go by. Marci needed guidance, some sort of instructions on how to adjust to this new normal of caretaking. For now, she thought, ice tea and chocolate cake would help soothe her soul.

After her weak moment with sugar, Marci made sure her mom was comfortable and went back to her bedroom for some much needed quiet. She grabbed her nail polish and gave herself a quick pedicure for her date tomorrow night. She didn't even know what that was anymore. Marci sat there and thought back to the day she ran into Dr. Hutchins and his son 'Hutch' Hutchins, an intern in Radiology.

"Marci, Marci," Dr. Hutchins bellowed from down the hall of the hospital. Turning around, Marci came to a complete stop and smiled. "Dr. Hutchins, how nice to see you again." Marci gave her favorite doctor and close family friend a hug and stepped back. "Marci, you remember my son, Hutch, don't you?"

Marci looked at Hutch recalling the few times they played together as children, and not particularly liking him either.

Marci nodded at Hutch and said, "Of course I remember; how are you doing Hutch?"

Hutch gave a dazzling smile to Marci and told her he was doing fine.

"Boy was his smile bright," she thought. "Must have just used those whitening teeth strips that are all the rage." Marci grinned at the thought. But, she had to admit, he was not hard on the eyes at all.

"It's been a few years since we've seen each other hasn't it?" he said.

"Yes, it has been." Marci answered.

"Do you have time to have coffee with an old friend," he asked.

"Well…" she hesitated, "I guess Mom will be alright for a little bit."

"I heard from Dad that Sylvia is doing as well as she possibly can."

"Yes, my mom is a fighter, that's for sure." Marci replied.

Marci kept glancing at him sideways as they walked in unison to the hospital cafeteria. It was almost crazy that they were so in sync with their steps. Marci paused in stride as Hutch opened the door to the cafeteria for her. They settled into a small table and Hutch got their coffee. Sipping slowly Marci noticed Hutch looking intently at her. She smiled and said, "Have I got something on my face?"

Hutch grinned, "Nooo, to be honest I just don't remember you being this pretty when we were younger."

"Seriously, Hutch did you just say that? What middle school kids look good during puberty? If I recall you were no catch with braces and skinny legs."

"Whoa Marci, I didn't mean to offend, what I meant and should have said was, you have become a really beautiful woman."

Marci grinned, "Okay, you saved yourself...truce?"

"Truce," he agreed.

From that moment on they clicked. Same beliefs, similar goals and both loved the mountains where you could renew your spirit when the world got crazy.

An hour passed in no time, and Hutch looked at his cell phone for the time and then checked one message. "I'm sorry Marci, I promised a couple of patients that I would come by and talk with their families; can we see each other again soon?"

Marci smiled and agreed as he entered her number into his phone and promised to call.

Two days later he called and they made a date for Saturday night dinner. Marci was in a slight panic of leaving her mom alone but Sylvia insisted she would be fine. So, with much trepidation, Marci agreed. So here she was the night before the date painting her toes...and thinking about what to wear for their dinner date.

Marci got off the bed and walked on her bare heels to the closet and with a quick hand pushed hanger after hanger checking out each item. Nothing, nothing, nothing, Marcia sighed to herself. What would she wear?

It would be rather cool so maybe boots, jeans and this beautiful blue shirt her mother had picked out for her would work. The shirt was a deep sapphire blue with silver buttons, a great contrast with her coloring. Problem solved. Marci stopped her pondering for just a moment when she heard a slight thump. What was that, she wondered.

Marci stepped out into the hall and barely heard her mom's whisper, "Help me Marci."

With those words Marci ran to her mom and helped her back into her recliner.

"Mom, what were you doing?"

Sylvia gave an impish but apologetic smile. "I was tired of sitting so I thought I'd go lie down for a few minutes and get my strength up. I guess I underestimated how tired I really was." For a moment she was frightened, she was not ready to lose her. Not now.

Marci helped her mom to her bed and got her tucked in and safe. "Now mom, ring this bell if you need to get up again so I can help you."

"Now I'm no invalid honey, just don't worry about me, I'll be good as new in the morning."

Marci looked at her mother, really looked at her face and saw the tired lines around her eyes and mouth. It broke her heart to see her vibrant, feisty mother become quiet and withdrawn.

"Mom, I know you'll be good as new but until then…ring this bell or I'll have to call the doctor to fuss at you."

Sylvia grinned at her daughter's spunk…she was one proud mom of her daughter's gutsiness, proof she came from good stock, southern stock that is.

Marci turned going back to her haven of comfort and solitude and to making her final decision on her outfit. She was still concerned about leaving her mom alone right now. Marci mulled that thought over as she looked at her choice.

Sylvia sat in her chair mulling thoughts over also, she was so afraid of being too much of a burden for Marci. Sylvia shuffled around a little bit trying to ease the pain in her hip that she had thought was arthritis but it wasn't. Her prognosis wasn't as good as she led Marci to believe, but it was her job as a mom to protect her daughter's heart. So, she saved her tears for when she was alone but when Marci was around, the happy face came out as chirpy as ever.

Hutch was excited about his date with Marci. Not only was she lovely, but smart and kind and had a country lilt to her voice that captivated him. At thirty two he was not playing games in dating, he knew the kind of woman he wanted, so after the first date if the urgency to see her again was not there, he wouldn't be back. But if it was..... .

Marci wore her black jeans and boots along with her lovely blue shirt and silver accessories and twirled in front of her mom.

"What do you think Mom?" she asked.

Sylvia whistled, "Honey you are gorgeous, and he won't be able to take his eyes off of you."

"Oh mom," Marci said with a sigh, "you are so prejudiced, but I love you for it."

Marci hugged her mom tight just as the doorbell rang.

"That's him," Sylvia squealed not so quietly. Marci gave her the 'shush' look and opened the door. Hutch was standing there looking quite handsome in his jeans and a tan corduroy jacket and held two bunches of hydrangeas. Smiling at Marci he walked in and went straight for Sylvia.

"Sylvia, it's been a few years hasn't it?" he asked as he leaned over to hug and hand her the flowers.

Sylvia laughed and her eyes danced, "Hutch, you were always the charmer, even before puberty!"

Hutch died laughing. "You're right Sylvia, it's the family curse."

"Sit down, sit down and tell me about yourself for just a minute."

Marci let them chat a minute as she got a couple of mason jars which was her favorite way of displaying cut flowers and filled them up with water and placed the hydrangeas in them. She picked up the jar and

121

carried it to the table next to her mom for her to enjoy.

"Now Marci, you and Hutch go on and I'll be fine. I have everything I need, my cell phone, TV clicker, my books, paper, pens and most of all, my Bible. I promise I will be fine." Marci looked apprehensive so Sylvia said, "Hutch, take her somewhere fancy and don't let her talk about me, hospitals or sickness."

"Mother," Marci exclaimed, "You are terrible!"

Hutch laughed his way out of the house. "I don't remember your mom being quite the character…has she always been that way?"

"More so now than ever, she doesn't want me to see her sad or in pain, so she becomes lively and talkative thinking it erases the evidence."

"Does it?" he asked.

Marci gave a half-way smile, "Not really, but it's so much better than living in constant negativity or complaints; that would be hard to handle."

Hutch opened the door for her and she slid in. He walked to his side and got in but before he started the car he looked over and said to her, "You look amazing tonight, thank you for having dinner with me." Before she could reply, he started the car and as he was backing out he looked at her and winked.

That did it! In that one second she knew. She had prayed and asked God to give her a sign of who she would marry. She specifically asked God that he wink at her, just like her dad did to her mom forty years ago.

The night was incredible, with fabulous food, conversation that flowed and never stopped, then the stop for coffee afterwards and another two hours of talking. Marci couldn't believe how much they had in common—but then, that's what she asked God for wasn't it.

Hutch got her home safely, and with a light kiss and a promise to call tomorrow, he was off. Marci walked in the house seeing her mom slumped over in the chair asleep.

"Bless her," Marci said under her breath as she woke her mom up to help her to bed.

"Sweetheart, how was it? Did y'all hit it off really well?"

"Mom, he winked."

Sylvia's eyes lit up remembering her own special wink years ago. "I guess we have a wedding to plan don't we."

Marci smiled and her eyes were bright, "I believe we do mom, Hutch just doesn't know it yet."

"Well honey, that's best with men...you have to let them know a little at a time, then in the end they think it was all their idea. And you know what a good woman does?" Marci shook her head no.

"What does a good woman do?" Marci asked.

"Why, she lets him think it was all his idea." Sylvia said.

Marci laughed, "Well that should be easy enough Mom."

With that last piece of advice from her mom, they both went to bed remembering their own special wink. Sylvia's eyes sprung with tears from the past, while Marci's eyes shone for the future.

Months passed as Hutch and Marci got closer, seeing each other exclusively. It was only six months into the relationship when Hutch dropped the "L" word. Totally unexpected on that particular fall day. He had talked her into zip lining in the North Georgia Mountains and Marci was a tad nervous...she preferred her feet on solid ground but he was up for an adventure, and being a good sport, she agreed.

After getting hitched up, Marci closed her eyes as the guy gave her a little shove, the ride was exhilarating and breathtaking all at once. Hutch was right behind her having just as much fun. It ended all too soon for them both. After getting out of the harnesses, she went in for a hug and kiss, and with that he cupped her face with his hands and said, "I love you Marci."

Marci looked into his eyes and said, "I've loved you since the wink."

Hutch looked confused, "What wink?"

She just laughed, "I'll tell you about it in forty years."

Hutch grabbed her around the waist and said, "I'll wait for it."

Sylvia knew the moment she walked in that Marci was different. "He said he loved you didn't he?" Marci nodded yes, saying, "How do you do that?"

Sylvia laughed, "When you have a daughter one day, you will just know. Now, when's the wedding?"

"Mom, he said he loved me, he didn't propose."

"Well, it doesn't hurt to get a jump on things, let's head to Wal-Mart and pick up a few Bridal magazines…we'll keep them hid until he proposes." Marci just laughed and decided to humor her mom, plus she did kinda want to see the latest bridal dresses.

Later that evening after they had drooled over the magazines, talked over all the details, imagined the wedding and snacked on junk food, Marci noticed her mom seemed weaker than usual.

"Hey mom, why don't we turn in a little early tonight, I'm feeling really tired."

Sylvia didn't argue like she normally did, she agreed. "Okay honey, goodnight."

Marci made a mental note to talk with Hutch about her concerns.

The next day Marci texted Hutch to meet for lunch at the hospital cafeteria. It was the best place to catch him for a few minutes between patients or reports.

"What's up Hon?" he asked.

"Its mom Hutch, she's getting weaker and you know she's had all the chemo her body can take."

Hutch leaned back in his chair as he rubbed his hand through his hair in frustration. He tugged at his lab coat trying to decide exactly what to say. Marci leaned over and grabbed his hand and with tears in her eyes she said, "I know."

"How do you know?" he asked.

"She's my mom, I just know."

No further words were needed, she felt comforted just being at his side.

The days blurred as Sylvia grew weaker and weaker. Hutch proposed where he said he loved her giving Marci the ring of her dreams. Sylvia was ecstatic and just planning the wedding gave her a strength they hadn't seen in a while.

The wedding venue was in the mountains, the leaves were glorious in their color and fall was such a perfect time for Marci & Hutch to say, "I do." Sylvia was in her element being dressed to the nines and bedazzled the masses with her gaunt but still beautiful smile. Marci looked stunning in her well fitted gown covered with ivory lace and pearls. Her blonde hair was a mass of curls pulled over to the side in a loose bun that held a flower. She wore her mom's veil that matched her gown perfectly. Hutch's eyes filled with tears as he saw his bride walk toward him, it was a moment that he would remember forever.

The entire day was a blessing. Marci wished it would never end but she was excited about the secret honeymoon he had planned. All he told her was to bring a little bit of everything for a week. Her luggage was packed and ready for whatever adventure he had in store.

Sylvia glowed the whole time. So proud, so happy, so full of love for her daughter and Hutch. He was the perfect son-in-law and she knew she'd be the perfect, non-interfering mother-in-law…on that one she grinned. She would at least try not to interfere.

The weeks flew by. Sylvia moved in with the happy couple kicking and screaming. That was the last thing she wanted to do. But, Hutch was firm that he would not allow her to be alone. Fall turned into winter and the Christmas holidays were warm and happy. The winter chill came and Sylvia's health took a downward spiral. Home health came around some but Marci insisted on doing for her mother.

On the first day of spring, in the month of March, Marci and Hutch were by her side. They knew death was near and Marci overcome with grief leaned over to her mother's ear and said, "Mom, it's okay to go, Hutch will take good care of me, I love you so much mom, I love you so much. Marci kept repeating her words as Hutch held onto her.

She didn't even realize tears were flowing as she spoke next to her mother's cheek. When Sylvia took her last breath, Marci pulled back and gasped…for on her mother's pillow were her own tears formed in the shape of a heart.

She just knew, as she rubbed her own swollen belly…

It was a mother's heart.

"The Lord does not look at the things man looks at.
Man looks at the outward appearance, but the Lord looks
at the heart." 1 Samuel 16:76

The Widow Wagon

Standing by her SUV, Joyce juggles her suitcase in one arm and camera along with her purse in the other. Setting them all down she opens the back of her car and begins to organize. Nineteen years has passed since her husband died, and the joy for her Lord and her life continues to mirror her soul. With a last deliberate shove, she rearranged the food box she had put in earlier and stood up to see Marlene driving up the driveway. Joyce grinned as Marlene jumped out of her car ready and raring to go. Marlene a widow for seven years never lost her joy nor her energetic excitement for life, she continues to shine, oh how she does shine.

"Be joyful always; pray continually; give thanks in all circumstances, for this is

God's will for you in Christ Jesus." -1 Thessalonians 5: 16-18

After loading her luggage and boxes, they grabbed a chair and waited. These two knew Modree all too well. They would have time for a glass of sweet tea and a short talk as they waited for widow number three to show up. Modree lost her husband five years ago, and the joy? Well, all I can say is she truly radiates with the joy of the Lord. Within minutes, she drives up smiling and happy, and why not, they were going on a road trip together in the 'Widow Wagon.'

What's the 'Widow Wagon' you ask?

It's a sign placed on the back window saying just that, 'Widow Wagon,' announcing to all who happen to glance at three God-loving women piled in a SUV headed for a fun destination.

Is it silly? Maybe. Is it fun? Absolutely. Does it make God smile? Without a doubt.

Do you have joy in the Lord? Do you glow with His love? Do your eyes sparkle with His reflection?

Joyce, Marlene and Modree have the joy, in spite of experiencing loss, difficulties, health issues, trauma, all that life can dish out. But, they know their Savior has a plan, a purpose for their lives and until they take their last breaths, they will live the joy.

These three ladies are my aunts. I am blessed.

I love their sense of fun, joy and laughter as they do life together in or out of the Widow Wagon.

"Rejoice in the Lord always. I will say it again: Rejoice!" - Philippians 4:4

What is the secret to their happy life? Gratitude. Gratitude begets joy.

Are they always happy? Heavens no! All flesh and blood have times of sadness, but these three women search for the positive and they find it, express it and are grateful for it.

So, if you're driving down the highway and see this sign in the back of an SUV, just give a big ol' smile, wave and maybe honk your horn... because you are passing the presence of Joy...the Joy of the Lord in their souls all bundled up in one special Widow Wagon. You will be blessed, I promise.

"May the God of hope fill you with all joy and peace as you trust in him, so that you may overflow with hope by the power of the Holy Spirit." -Romans 15:13

"Whenever you feel unloved, unimportant or insecure,
remember to whom you belong."
Ephesians 2:19-22

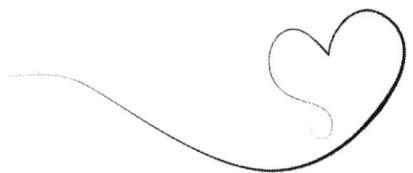

Digging Up Sisters

Shifting herself up in bed, Sara heard deep guttural cries, the kind that come from the depths of your soul. It was then she realized those were from her own throat. Even in sleep, the pain was continuous and lonely, a persistent reminder of her loss.

Just a few weeks ago she and Kara were next-door-neighbors, best friends, prayer warriors...they became sisters by choice. The first day they met, Sara was outside gardening in her flower beds when Kara came up and introduced herself as the new neighbor. First, their names rhymed and that made them laugh, they were the same age, had children in college, each loved gardening and loved Jesus. Their friendship was undoubtedly a God-thing and they became tight friends, a "sista'hood" that both cherished.

Sara remembered the day they joined gardening forces. Their lawns connected beautifully, so began the process of making a flower garden that flowed into both yards. Truly, from spring through fall the garden was a stunning, fanciful work of art. How they loved planning, digging, fertilizing and picking flowers every week for their table. Kara favored the reds, pinks and purples but she especially adored the bold reds, where as Sara was drawn to the more bashful yellow, white and blue flowers.

They decided to add arbors, then a primitive sign or two popped up. Both loved the whimsical country style...it was in their blood and wildflowers mimicked that style as they swayed in the garden. Each morning they would meet on the memory bench, a special seat honoring the life of Sara's daughter who passed away a few years ago in a car accident. Gardening soothed the soul for Sara and having Kara was a blessing. They would drink coffee in the early morning before tending to the flowers...then, late in the afternoon when the sun had almost disappeared they met again for iced tea to enjoy the fruits of their labor.

For ten lovely years they were a sista'hood trolling with the love of the Lord in their garden. If the flowers could talk they would share Kara and Sara's many heart-to-heart talks that encompassed all of life's tearful disappointments, its craziness, endearing love and of course, friendships. But no more.

Sara gathered herself together to push through another day. She looked out the window and saw how the garden needed tending to... it looked sad, mirroring how she felt. Kara was with Jesus now. It happened so quickly, feeling sick, tests, diagnosis and a vicious, unrelenting disease that took her in six weeks. The whys were constant...the answer slow in coming.

They hardly had time to say good-bye and with flowers picked from their garden she sprinkled them across her grave.

The months passed, the weeds grew, and the flowers hardly bloomed. Sara begged God for comfort...but, the underlying anger was blocking it and she knew that, but releasing meant reality and she wasn't ready to let go.

Weeks later, weary from the load she carried, losing her daughter and her best friend was too much to carry anymore. She fell to her knees and asked God to forgive her for her anger, for holding on and asked for peace. Immediately, the load lifted and the fog cleared...Kara was now locked safely in the pulse of Sara's veins pumping continuous memories of their love for gardening.

After Christmas Sara began to plan again. It was difficult at first, but then she allowed her excitement to grow. She needed to bring life back to the garden and to herself. Spring could not get here fast enough and when it arrived the spade came out and weeds disappeared. Slowly, flowers began seeking the sun the weeds had denied and color emerged.

Sara smiled more. Flowers made her happy. She carried on the gardening with Kara always near. The flowers frolicked in the breeze and the morning coffee and afternoon tea were still sipped slowly on the memory bench, but it was she and God now enjoying the view and at times lively banter.

One morning Sara walked out while the dew was still shimmering on the petals of her prized Black-Eyed Susans her favorite perennial. They brought her so much joy as she eyed her huge patch of bright yellow...which reminded her of little beaming faces.

Sara stepped into her gardening shed and gathered her gloves, shears and a bucket of water from the spigot to hold the flowers until she could arrange them for the table. Sara gasped as she gazed upon her Black-Eyed Susans, for there in the middle of all the yellow splendor was one amazingly red daisy...tall, glorious and happy. It was Kara's love peeking through dressed in her favorite color!

Sara gasped, letting the tears roll; thanking God for the gift...such a personal sweet gift from Him that went straight to her heart. The splendid red daisy was a reminder to her that amongst all the heartbreak of loss in this world, the Son will break through and there will be life again.

"I sought the Lord, and He heard me,
and delivered me from all my fears." Psalm 34:4

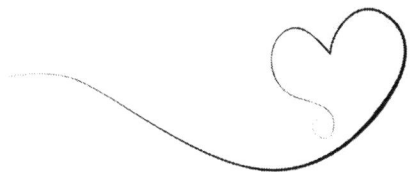

Crazy Love

Rolling her eyes to the back of her head as she had just glanced at the calendar for the month of February and glaring back at her was the 14th, the LOVE day. Groaning she threw herself backwards onto the bed reliving the other three previous months of pure agony. Thanksgiving…no date to the family dinner, Christmas… no date to the family dinner, New Year's Eve…no date to her friend's party and now apparently no date, no candy, no flowers, no nothing. Annie glanced at her cell phone for the time, 7:00 p.m. so she would give herself ten minutes for a pity party then get ready for the 8:00 p.m. youth party she was in charge of.

Annie laid on her bed with a trickle of tears falling out totally messing up her mascara. Both her sisters were happily married, and every phone call or lunch date was the continual question, "Have you met anyone lately?" Annie groaned again reliving her same answer each time…No. "Really," she thought, "how do you meet men when your life revolves around youth?" Annie looked at her cell phone again and realized more than ten minutes were up and she needed to get ready. Grabbing her leggings, boots and a fabulous sweater that her sister, Amanda bought her for Christmas she headed to the bathroom for a quick shower and make-up redo.

Forty minutes later she was headed to the church fellowship hall for a meeting with the parents while the youth played basketball. She loved being the youth pastor for now. She loved kids. This was, however, just a part-time job until her Masters was completed in three more months. She actually wanted to teach Bible in a Christian school, that way she got to be with kids as she taught the book she loved. A win-win career, but for now she needed to stay focused on the kids she loved and the parents who loved them.

Annie entered the church looking fresh and lively. Her sandy-colored hair was pulled over to the side almost touching her shoulder. Her big-brown eyes were always highlighted with mascara and she loved wearing coral lip gloss. She never considered herself a beauty, but more in the cute category. Waving to the parents as she walked towards them, she pulled out her clipboard for them to sign and update any information before the meeting started. Annie looked around, chatting with the different moms and dads when she noticed a new, ruggedly handsome man sitting alone.

Annie went over and introduced herself. "Hi, I'm Annie, the youth pastor and you are?"

Sam stood up and replied, "I'm Sam Arnold, we moved here from Kentucky recently and I wanted my brother, Caleb to be involved with a group of good kids." Annie's heart lurched, apparently he was taking care of his kid brother? What a great guy to do that.

"Tell me about your brother Sam." Annie said.

"Well," Sam grinned, "He's your typical teen, Caleb is a junior in high school, does well in his studies, is a great athlete and of course, likes the girls. He is a bit overwhelmed though right now. Our Dad left a few years ago, leaving mom to finish raising me and when she died six months ago, I took over to finish raising my little brother. Although, 'raising' is really not the correct term, maybe more 'overseeing' his choices." Sam grinned.

Annie grinned back, telling him she enjoyed speaking with him and that she'd make sure Caleb met everyone. Just a bit rattled, Annie went over the rest of the spring schedule with the parents, answered questions, told a couple of 'youth' stories about their kids, keeping the parents laughing and then dismissed with prayer.

Sam walked back over to her, "You are a great story-teller Annie I was quite impressed." "Oh don't be, I just love making whatever situation goes on come alive...I guess that's why I'm going into teaching." "What will you teach?" Sam inquired. Annie grinned, "High School Bible is what I hope to teach, but I'll be qualified to teach other subjects also." Sam grinned, "Well, it was really nice meeting you Annie, I hope to see you again soon." Annie smiled back as she shook his hand thinking, "I hope so too, Sam."

Sam walked away totally 'smitten' as his mom would say. She was his heart and not quite sure why he knew that...he just did. He opened his car door when Caleb appeared from the church gym, "Ready Sam?" he asked. "Sure, get in." he replied.

Sam turned to his brother and asked, "How do you like Annie?"

"She's great...kind of like having a sister, definitely the girl-next-door type."

"You mean the kind you take home to meet your mom kind of girl" Sam said.

"Yep, that's the kind, why do you ask?" Caleb grinned as he looked at his brother.

Sam ignored that question.

At twenty-nine Sam was a neat guy, at least to his brother. Very responsible, a go-getter in his career choice of construction. He could build anything, and his goal was to open his own company. Sam majored in Business and knew at some point he would combine his love for building with his knowledge of opening his own company. Caleb always looked up to his brother and envied his strong build that the women seemed to like. But, his brother never seemed to notice the women, his eyes were fixed on the completion of whatever project he was on. Caleb however, was a bit scrawny, not so wide in the shoulders. He was tall, thin and fun, he loved making people laugh and was always the life of a party. They were a great compliment to each other, both had always made their mama proud.

Annie gathered her papers and locked up the church. Heading home she opened her sunroof and let the night air soothe her thoughts. It was a great night with the parents, all were wonderful and supportive. But, her thoughts kept wandering back to Sam Arnold. She was definitely attracted to him but knew she would not see him often so she just better put him out of her mind. Better said than done she mused.

The next day Sam arrived at work at 6 a.m. to look at the plans for the new home he was in charge of. This was his biggest one yet and he wanted to do well.

"Hello Mr. Taylor, how are you doing this morning?" Sam inquired as he shook the owner's hand.

"Great Sam, and please call me Thomas."

"Alright Thomas, are you ready for us to break ground?"

"Ready."

The day was long but extremely productive. The home was underway and Sam couldn't have been more pleased with that day's work. Arriving home late that night, he couldn't help but think of Annie and wondering how her day went. He also wished he could get her number, then realized it was on the form he filled out for Caleb. Sam pulled his jeans off the chair and checked his back pocket and there it was with her name, Annie Carroll, with her address and cell number. He quickly looked at the clock noting the time and thought he'd go for it.

"Hello."

"Annie, this is Sam Arnold we met last night, I'm Caleb's brother."

Annie smiled as she talked, "of course I remember you Sam, so glad to hear from you."

"Well, I'll be frank Annie, I would love to take you to dinner and get to know you better."

"I'd like that Sam." Annie replied.

"Do you have plans for Friday night? Maybe dinner at the new Italian restaurant in town."

"Friday would be great." Annie said.

"I'll pick you up at 6p.m." Sam said.

"But you don't know where I live."

"Oh but I do, I have your address and my GPS...we're good."

Annie hung up and squealed. He felt it too, she thought. She quickly ran to the closet looking for something to wear. It was Wednesday, so she only had two days to figure it out. It would take two days just to find her clothes, some were dirty and needed washing, some on the chair next to the bed, some thrown in the closet. Oh, she needed to get organized but that just wasn't her best quality. Annie groaned at all she had to do in 48 hours...well at least this motivated her.

Friday came quickly, and Annie had washed, hunted down, and put away all her clothes. Her small bungalow that she inherited from her grandmother was spotless. She kept her thick hair down this time, it was naturally curly and bounced as she walked. She chose a coral top that she loved, very chic with a little lace to go along with her leggings and boots. Her final touch was gold hoop earrings and a final swipe of lip gloss. Turning to and fro in front of her full length mirror she thought, "Well, it's as good as it's going to get."

The doorbell rang and Annie tried to walk slowly to answer it, "Hi Sam, come on in," she said.

Sam walked in looking quite handsome in his jeans, boots and solid blue shirt. But, he was the one that sucked in his breath, she was lovely and he said so.

"Wow Annie, you look amazing."

Blushing, Annie didn't quite know what to say, but "thank you Sam."

"Ready?"

"Let me grab my wrap and purse." She said.

The ride was wonderful, there was never a pause...conversation flowed easily and in thirty minutes they both felt quite at ease. Jumping out of his truck, Sam ran around to her side and opened her door.

Annie gave him another bonus point for that. The other was for picking her up and not asking her to meet him somewhere. She had grown weary of other men asking her to do that. She knew it was probably safer but where was the chivalry? It didn't seem to exist anymore.

Once seated she had Sam talking about his life, his aspirations, dreams and goals. He talked twenty minutes before he realized he was doing all the talking. "How do you do that?" he asked.

"Do what?" she grinned.

"Get me to talk so much." Sam laughed.

"It comes with the territory of working with youth, and besides your life is much more interesting than mine."

Sam laughed, "My life is the same, work then more work at home to prepare for the next day, then bed. I'm actually pretty boring."

Annie's gaze fell on his eyes, "Not to me you're not." Sam reached over and picked up her hand and stroked it ever so lightly.

Her heart skipped a beat. Could you possibly fall in love within three hours? Was that possible? If it were possible, then that was exactly what she had done. "God, she said, I know you're in control so please let me know if I've gone crazy...or if I'm just falling crazy in love."

Sam never let go of her hand except to pay for the dinner. Even when she offered to pay half, he just gave her 'the look' of absolutely not and they left. Driving home, Sam kept his arm on top of hers and it felt as natural as if they had done this all their lives. He had no doubt, she was the girl for him. Now, to see how she felt.

Coming to a stop at her driveway, Annie asked him to come in and Sam happily agreed. It was two in the morning before he left, they had covered every subject, every scenario, swapped family stories and laughed continuously. Annie never kissed on the first date, but this time was different. It wasn't a first date, it was the beginning of a lifetime.

Caleb had come in from his high school football game and party afterwards about midnight and Sam wasn't home. Not too concerned, he grabbed a coke and watched some TV. waiting up for Sam. The key turned in the door causing a couple of clicks and Hutch sat up waiting for his brother to come in.

"Hey bro, where have you been?" Caleb asked.

"Been out on a date." Sam responded.

"Date...you?"

"Really Sam, you had a date?"

"Yes, I had a date."

"But you never date."

"I do now." Sam stated with a grin.

"Who with?" Caleb asked.

"Your Youth Pastor, Annie."

Caleb leaned back on the sofa and plastered a big ole' grin on his face.

"Great choice...definitely a 'mom approved' girl" Caleb winked.

Sam threw a pillow at his little brother thinking he sure was glad he had Caleb around...otherwise, the nights would probably be a bit long.

Annie called her sister, Amanda, to share that she had found her soulmate at least, that was how she felt at the moment. Amanda screamed into the phone, "That's wonderful Annie...tell me everything."

Annie told her everything except she forgot to tell her his last name.

"So sis, is he just Sam or does he have a last name?" she giggled.

"Oh sorry, his name is Arnold, Sam Arnold."

Amanda sat in silence.

"Why so quiet Amanda?" Annie asked.

"Was his mom and dad's name Sarah and Steven Arnold?"

"Yes, Why?"

"Well the Arnolds were known for their generosity in Kentucky, they were quite wealthy and loved helping people. But, Mr. Arnold's generosity also extended itself to young, pretty women. He had an ongoing affair that ended their 25 years of marriage. In Sarah's grief she became very ill and died a year later leaving her boys alone. Their father, I understand tried but never fully reclaimed his relationship with his sons. However Steven Arnold surfaced later on the arm of my husband's aunt, Lily Canter. She is now a part of our family Annie.

Annie sat stunned. Absolutely speechless. "What would she say to Sam?"

"Why didn't you tell me Amanda?"

"Annie, I've probably mentioned Aunt Lily before, but there was no reason to mention him."

"You're right, does his dad live near here?"

"Yes, about ten minutes down the road from you actually, in the Country Clubs private homes."

Annie just sat on her bed and tried to absorb all the details. What would she do? Or rather, what could she possibly say to Sam, especially since they have no relationship and now his dad was practically in her family?

Just breathe she told herself. This was going to take a lot of prayer and wisdom to handle.

That night Sam came over for dinner. Annie cooked his favorite meal of rib-eye steak, and of course ended it with fudge cake. Sam practically rolled from the table to the sofa.

"Annie, if I ate like this every night, you would have a hefty fella to deal with." He said laughingly.

Annie grinned, "I think I could live with that."

After a time of catching up and watching the news together, Annie thought she would venture the subject of his dad.

"Sam, why don't you ever mention your dad?"

She could tell he was rolling his thoughts around in his head.

"Well, after he left my mom for another woman, I decided that I would leave him. He tried to contact me some, but I never returned his calls or texts. I've forgiven him, I just have no desire to see him."

Annie sat for a while mulling over his words then asked, "Do you know where your father lives?"

"I suppose he still lives in Kentucky, why?"

"Well, I was telling my sister, Amanda about you. She asked if you were Steven and Sara Arnold's son from Kentucky, and I said yes. Amanda got real quiet after she told what she knew about your family and then shocked me when she shared the news that your dad lives here, just ten minutes away in the Country Club with Amanda's husband's cousin, Lily Canter"

Annie let that absorb for just a minute. Sam just sat there quite dumbfounded.

"Sam, are you okay." He shook his head yes.

"Well, I suppose it was inevitable that I would see him at some point, God doesn't let you go too long without facing your issues. But, right now, the issue at hand is Valentine's Day not my father," he said as he kissed her.

"So dress up, everything is a surprise."

February 14 couldn't get here soon enough. She had spent the entire day having a mani-pedi, then hair swooped up with tendrils hanging down. Her dress was black with a high neck but lower in the back. Annie practically glowed the entire day.

Sam arrived with two dozen coral roses, he remembered her absolute favorite color. She was thrilled. Sam loved and appreciated her response by leaning in with a kiss. Annie quickly put the roses in water and looked back at Sam dressed so handsomely in a black suit. You look amazing in that suit so we need a 'selfie' for memories. Annie grabbed her cell phone and took a picture of them. Sam just laughed at how women loved to take pictures.

At the restaurant, Sam had planned a quiet but romantic dinner for them both. He was able to get an out of the way table that overlooked the city lights. A candle was lit on the table and the night was perfect. Sam knew without a doubt this was his girl for life. He fell in love with Annie the minute he saw her and his heart grew deeper in love. It had only been six weeks, which was crazy he knew but wasn't crazy love the best kind? Sam pulled out a beautiful oval diamond ring set in platinum and surrounded by smaller diamonds and proposed at dinner.

Annie gasped at the ring, and said yes. It was a surreal moment she would treasure always. She knew he was her forever, she just didn't know it would be tonight. After a few minutes of staring at her ring, leaning in and kissing her fiancé and discussing their future together, she saw a man and woman coming towards them. Sam couldn't see but when he heard the voice he quickly turned around.

"Dad?" Sam said.

"Hi son, how are you doing?" Not wanting to make a scene, he replied "Really well," as he stood up to look him squarely in the face. His dad turned to Lily and introduced her to his son, then he looked at Annie.

Sam said, "This is my fiancé Annie, we just got engaged." Annie shook his hand warmly and also Lily's who of course looked very familiar to her. Lily started to speak but thought better of it.

"Congratulations to you both."

"Thank you."

"Sam, do you think we could meet this week and talk, I would really like to share some things with you in private."

Sam struggled for a second, then said, "yes, Dad that would be good."

They shook hands, Steven also leaned in and hugged Annie saying, "I'm glad he has you."

Annie teared up for several reasons but the one that made her so proud was Sam who was willing to try and repair his relationship with his dad.

Sam pulled her close, he and Caleb now had a family.

And Annie? Well, she had a dinner date for every Thanksgiving, Christmas, New Years and Valentines. All was well in her crazy love soul.

"Do justly, love mercy, walk humbly." Micah 6:8

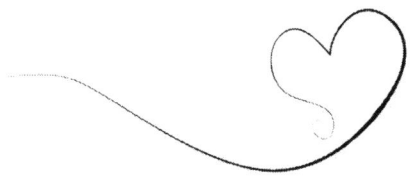

A Summer Of Ashes To Beauty

Jena leaned back into her red beach chair soaking in the salty air. Pushing her cheap but stylish sunglasses onto her head, she took in the fascinating pelicans as they soared then plundered into the ocean gulping fish. Jena knew how the fish felt being swallowed into the unknown. She felt her body tense as she related to the pelicans. Quickly, Jena pulled her glasses back down and taking another breath, re-directed her thoughts into prayer.

Dear God...I need peace. Annie is in your hands. Guide her in the right direction as she seeks Mike to be her husband. Amen.

Jena croaked on that prayer. Mike is not who they had hoped she would marry. Jena wanted a 'normal' son-in-law who loved Jesus, maybe even a Preacher. But instead, they got Prisoner #908080 named Mike who was released to a half-way house a few months ago. Addicted to cocaine, he stole constantly to fund his addiction after he put in a full days work as a master plumber. He made really good money in his field, but it wasn't enough. Annie, fell in love during one of his times out and when he went back to prison she was his constant advocate. Jena worried herself sick. Would Annie be sucked into his life?

It would be a miracle if Mike became a committed Christian, never straying back to the 'other side'. God is a very big God...it could happen, but would it?

Mike was sitting in the half-way house reading his Bible. He had accepted Christ four years ago while in prison. He took every Bible course available, journaling became his outlet and prayer his passion. He had three more weeks in the half-way house and was doing amazingly. He acquired a plumbing job that made fair money and Annie who'd waited patiently for him to get out was also trusting God that all would be well as he re-entered the 'real-world.'

Thinking about Annie, he worried if he was being fair. He was 35 and alone. His family consisted of four stair-step brothers, each having a different, non-existent dad. His mother was a throwback of the sixties, bleached blonde hair, t-shirts and at 55 still smoked marijuana. He had started stealing at 15, small things at first, then built up over time to cars and breaking into homes. He never hurt people, physically at least, he just hurt himself. Then came Annie...sweet and caring, innocent of people like him; she was different, her face always had joy. At 29, she was waiting for his complete release...would he disappoint her? Could he live up to God's best for him?

"Mike," his roommate said, "you're wanted on the phone." Mike pulled himself away from his thoughts and responded with a wave of thanks.

"Hello," Mike said hoping it was Annie. "Mike, this is Paul your Parole Officer. I have good news for you, this is your last day at the half-way house...they need your bed for another guy. Call Annie and have her pick you up at noon tomorrow." A few more instructions, then Mike was sitting on the steps in a cold sweat. This was it.

Jena came home from the beach for a quick shower. Her phone rang just as she stepped into her ice-cold condo. "Hello," Jena said shivering.

"Mom, it's Annie...I just got the call, Mike is getting out tomorrow. I have to be there at noon to pick him up."

"Mom...Mom....are you there?"

"Yes, sweetheart, I'm here." "I'm just a bit stunned that's all." Switching ears she hurried out to the deck where the air was warmer. "What's your plan after the pick-up?"

"I'm taking Mike to Pastor Ryan's house until we get married, then he'll move into my home."

Silence.

"Mom," Annie pleaded, "He's a new man in Christ...give him a chance."

"We will Annie, I promise." Jena said. Easing to her knees she cried out. God filled her with warmth as He whispered into her heart, "Jena, they are mine."

The wedding was beautiful. From ashes to beauty...Mike was redeemed.

God healed his addiction to cocaine, and restored to him another family...Annie's faimly.

His zeal for God is evident in their new ministry. Mike shares his testimony and hundreds of inmates have accepted Jesus.

And Jena? She's back on the beach watching the birds; seeing her life shift. Instead of being swallowed up...she is like the pelican...fishing; except she fishes for beauty found in the ashes through Pelican's Prison Ministry.

God is a BIG God.

"Blessed is she who has believed that the Lord would fulfil his promises to HER." Luke 1:45

Heavenly Recess

Fourteen year old Lauren leaned her head back on her pillow. Her once beautiful face now drained of all youth, her lips no longer rosy but raw and split. Lauren shut her eyes for a brief moment in hopes the nausea would leave. That was not to be as she leaned over her bed, dry-heaving so hard that the blood vessels had begun to burst in the whites of her eyes.

Struggling for thoughts or at least a thought to come to her mind, Lauren stared at her Bible laying on her nightstand. She focused on the worn, brown leather that covered the pages containing all the promises, love and understanding that her beloved Father said was hers.

But, "were they hers?" Speaking out loud in a hoarse whisper, her Father promised her healing, He promised her that He would be there, and He promised her peace that passed all understanding. But did those promises mean she would receive all that now?

Exhaustion shook her pencil-thin frame. Lauren rolled over and allowed sleep to take her briefly out of reality. She fell into a dreamless state, void of everything except the thought of living.

And living was what Lauren wanted to do.

"Knock, knock," her mom called out as she was opening Lauren's bedroom door a couple of hours later. "Sweetheart, it's time to take your meds."

Lauren slowly opened her eyes to focus on her mom's concerned face. Worry lines had permanently etched themselves deeper on her forehead and her eyes were glassy from lack of sleep.

"Hey Mom, are you okay?" Lauren whispered.

Maggie just smiled at her daughter saying, "Wonderful, and it's getting better, because I've got my cup of coffee and I'm with my favorite girl."

Lauren swallowed the three pills and snuggled further into the covers. Eek! She suddenly screamed and then her shock turned to young girlish giggles.

"Mom look." Lauren dug deep into the covers and pulled out a stuffed rat; compliments of her baby brother, no less. He was always trying to make her laugh, at least these last few months anyway. She stared sadly at the stuffed animal. "Mom?"

"Hmmm," she answered as she sipped her strong brew.

"I had a weird thought just as I was going to sleep. When something like that happens, could that be God speaking to me?"

"Well, I find that sometimes when God speaks, He does so in a way that leaves no doubt it's from Him."

Lauren lay quiet and still, pondering what her mother had said.

Maggie gently urged her saying, "Sweetheart do you feel God shared something with you?"

Lauren nodded her head yes.

"Would you like to tell me?"

In that moment, Lauren's words tumbled out just as God had spoken them to her.

"Do you remember Lauren when you were a little girl and how much you loved recess at school? How every day recess was the highlight of your day and sometimes the teacher would pick you and another student to receive recess early. Are you remembering how that felt? The thrill? You got to play longer than your friends for that day."

"Yes, I remember."

"Well, that's how life is for children at times. For some, class is dismissed early and they get the thrill of recess before their friends. For others, class is not over for many, many years and their recess comes later."

Lauren looked over at her mother who had tears in her eyes.

"Mom, I always loved recess."

"I know, sweetheart," she said as she reached over and touched her daughter's face, "I know."

"The Lord is close to the brokenhearted.
He rescues those who's spirits are crushed." Psalm 34:18

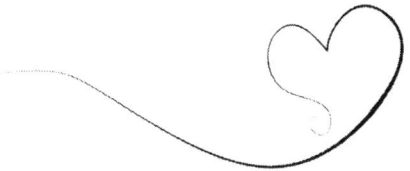

Not Those Church Ladies Again....

Glossy coral was today's choice of color for her summer toes as she wiggled them dry in front of the oscillating fan from her mother's closet. They were just about dry when she jumped up and walked on her heels to the closet pondering on what she should wear for tonight's date. She yanked hanger after hanger across the rod thinking, no…no…no…maybe….yes this dress could be what she should wear. Pulling the sundress off the plastic red hanger and holding it up to her neck, Annie decided it brought out the green in her eyes, not to mention it had been her mother's favorite.

Annie leaned against her antique wardrobe thinking of her mom who had passed away over a year ago. She so longed to share these moments with her but it was not to be. With a big sigh, Annie plopped back onto her bed to check her toes one more time when she heard her dad ringing the hand bell.

"I'll be right there Pops."

Annie swung her legs around to the floor and took off down the hall to the side porch where her dad sat with his foot in a cast.

"What's up? Do you need something?"

He just grinned and grabbed her hand. "I wanted to tell you that Judy called from the church and she's bringing over a casserole for dinner tonight."

"Not the church ladies again!" Annie cried out in dismay.

"Well…not ladies in the plural sense, just one lady…Judy."

"Pops, I'm perfectly capable of making your dinner, we certainly don't need one of the church ladies to bring food."

Annie rolled her eyes as she thought about the first time she met these ladies from her parent's church. It was a few days after her mom had been buried and the doorbell rang with three single church ladies toting casseroles to give their condolences. Pops was totally oblivious that they were all single and dressed to the nines. But not her! Heavens no...she had heard all about these casserole toting ladies and she was not about to let her dad become prey to one.

"Annie, her dad prodded, I told Judy you had a date tonight so I thought it would be nice if she stayed and ate with me."

Annie groaned...loudly.

"Really Pops, Really?"

"Well, it would be nice to have some company my age," he said with a wink.

Annie studied her handsome dad. At sixty, he was still quite the looker with dark hair on the top and silver filtered on the sides. Her mom had always loved his dimples when he smiled...she said that's when she fell in love with him. Annie could see why, with his fine-looking features and sincere charm, he was definitely a contender with women.

"Pops, will you be okay while I go out tonight? I mean, should I leave you alone with this casserole toting church lady? She said with a grin.

As he was laughing at her words, he rearranged his broken ankle on the footstool and replied, "I think I can handle the situation...besides, I like Judy, we have great conversations and we do have a lot in common."

"Well, I know the Bible talks about taking care of the widows and orphans but I don't think I've ever read where the church ladies were supposed to take care of the widowers!" and with that, Annie giggled and ran off as the pillow missed hitting her behind.

With a final touch of lip gloss and a quick glance in the mirror she was ready to take off and meet Zeke. They had met at a church conference held on St. Simon's Island a month ago. He was a pastor of a small church not far from her hometown and Annie was a therapist for troubled teens in her county's court system. They immediately hit it off. His humor drew her in as well as his charm. Her mother always said it was better to have a man who could make you laugh through the good and bad times…life was easier that way.

Annie jumped in her red jeep, pulled her hair back in a ponytail, put on her sunglasses and headed to the Mexican restaurant for dinner on the patio. As she drove up, she caught his eye and waved. He walked over and opened her door, giving her a quick peck on the cheek.

"Glad you're here Annie," he said in his most sincere southern drawl.

"Me too Zeke."

Two hours later they were still sitting on the patio talking. The sun had started to drift down and the tiny patio lights came on giving the area a soft glow.

"So, how is your dad doing since he broke his foot?"

"Well tonight he is doing fabulously since the church lady came with her casserole to visit," she said grinning but with a hint of sarcasm.

"Church lady?"

"Oh yes, the church lady." Annie replied.

"And why are you against her?" he asked.

"I'm not exactly against her, she continued to say, I'm just not thrilled that these single women showed up at our door soon after my mom died with a casserole in hand giving us their condolences."

"Well, that does sound terrible for concerned women to cook up food, travel in their car, and say how sorry they are for your loss…what church did these horrible women come from?"

Annie glared at him.

Zeke however, doubled over in laughter.

"You should see your face right now Annie…I think you need a therapist!" Oh wait, you are one!"

Annie had to laugh at herself.

"Okay you win. I know I'm being a bit much about this, but really Zeke, I feel like they are after my dad and I'm not ready to hand him over yet."

Zeke leaned over and grabbed her hand. "Now we're getting to the raw spot Annie, it's you who are not ready...right?"

Tears welled up in her eyes and Zeke tightened his grip as she nodded yes.

"You know Annie, whether you are 28 like we are or 98, it's still hard to let go of the people we love whether it's from death or new relationships."

Annie nodded afraid to say a word for fear of the ugly cry would descend upon her.

"You know, Zeke continued, I lost my dad a few years back from heart disease and my mom has been all alone, I guess you could say she is one of those, 'church ladies' you're talking about."

Annie grinned.

"She's 58, still young and healthy and has the best outlook on life and of course, I am prejudiced but I think she is quite beautiful."

"I'm sure she is Zeke, but how would you feel about her remarrying?"

Zeke leaned back in his chair and thought for a moment... "Well, it has been three years since dad died and depending on the type of man, and how happy she is, I think I would be fine."

Annie just sat for a moment absorbing all that Zeke had said. He did make perfect sense, and she knew he was right, but it was hard to let go.

Zeke leaned over and lightly kissed her, he knew where his heart was going and just prayed hers was going the same place.

Annie caught her breath at the kiss, it took her off guard. She looked at Zeke and knew. Her mother had always said she would know...and she did. But, how did he feel?

Zeke walked her to her jeep and helped her in. He had a hard time letting her drive off but finally he backd away after they promised each other another date two nights later.

It was almost midnight when Annie arrived home, and the family room light was still on and the church lady's car was still in the driveway.

"Oh great, she thought, I hope this won't be awkward."

Annie walked in as they were still drinking coffee and laughing.

"Hello sweetheart," her dad said, "you remember Judy don't you?"

"Absolutely Judy, very nice to see you again."

Judy smiled and said, "I had such a nice time visiting your dad tonight, he certainly kept me in stitches with all his stories."

Stan looked over at Judy and winked.

Annie saw the wink and just died.

"Well, so glad y'all had a good time, I think I'll go on to bed as she leaned over to kiss her dad on the cheek."

Annie scurried off quickly...hoping her face didn't give her away. Was her dad really liking the church lady? It certainly appeared that way after she witnessed the wink. This was just too much to think about, so Annie changed into her PJ's and climbed into bed. One last thought made her grab her Bible and see if she could find a verse about those church ladies taking care of widowers. She just shut her Bible and giggled.

Zeke could not get Annie off his mind. She was as lovely on the inside as she was on the outside. Everything about her was attractive to him...even her crazy thoughts about the casserole toting church ladies. He just shook his head and laughed. As a pastor though, he knew as zany as it was to him, to Annie it was real and he was determined to help her through this.

Two nights passed slowly but finally their date night arrived and Zeke had made plans to pick up Annie at her house. He wanted to meet her dad and form his own opinions. Zeke drove up to the old country place which was well kept and loaded with personality along with a porch appearing to be twelve feet deep with plenty of rocking chairs to sit in. Zeke climbed the steps and instantly saw Stan, Annie's dad.

"Hello sir, I'm Zeke."

"Well hello Zeke, I'm Annie's dad, Stan," he said with warmth as he shook his hand.

"Have a seat, pointing to another rocking chair, "Annie will be out here shortly.""

For about twenty minutes he and Stan had a great conversation that flowed easily almost like they had known each other for years. Zeke felt great about her Dad and planned to tell her.

Annie walked out letting the screen door slam and both men's heads turned around. Zeke's eyes looked appreciatively at Annie's outfit, noting how wonderful she always dressed. Classy and comfortable…his favorite style for a woman.

She walked toward her dad and gave him a kiss, then just as easily stepped next to Zeke and grabbed his hand. Stan saw his daughter look up at Zeke with such ease and admiration in her eyes and for a moment, he felt the profound loss of his wife and their love.

Zeke put his arm around Annie's waist and guided her down the steps and to his car. He opened the door and she slid into the passenger side appreciating the soft leather seats and clean interior. After Zeke settled in and they clicked their seatbelts, then headed north toward town.

"Where are we going?" Annie asked, but not really caring. She was just enjoying being with him.

"I'm taking you to therapy," he said with a twinkle in his eye.

"What! I don't need therapy," she retorted.

"Trust me."

"I don't know if I can trust a pastor," she said laughing.

"Well, tonight you're going to find out if you can." Zeke leaned over and grabbed her hand and gave her a wink.

"Yep, she thought, I am totally undone…he is 'the one.'

Zeke drove toward town then when on through the town winding around the back roads until he pulled up to the sweetest looking cottage she had ever seen.

"Oh Zeke, how charming this is. Who does this cottage belong to?"

"It belonged to my grandmother who left it to my mom, but after dad died it was just too painful for her to visit here and well, I come up here to write my sermons."

Annie turned around looking in all directions at the beauty of the surroundings. It possessed all that makes life captivating, a pond, hills, and wild flowers growing in clusters and underneath a huge oak tree was a swing. Perfection.

Zeke watched Annie take it all in. "So, he said, does this place make you feel like you've had therapy for the soul?"

Annie turned around almost breathless, "Absolutely, I feel revitalized and we've only been here a few minutes."

Zeke guided her to the inside of the cottage where earlier he had brought over lunch and they sat on the screened porch eating, chatting and enjoying nature's beauty. After, they were finished Zeke cleared his throat and began to explain his feelings for her.

"I know we haven't known each other long, but for me you're the girl I've been waiting for."

Annie sucked in her breath...he did feel the same!

"She looked up into his eyes and said, "I am the girl for you," and sealed their commitment with a kiss.

***

Several hours later, Zeke and Annie were headed back to her home when she thought she might check on her dad. Grabbing her cell phone out of her bag, she punched in his number.

"Hello."

"Pops, it's me...are you doing okay?"

"I'm great, he said, it's just me and Judy enjoying the day on the porch. Are you headed home?" he asked.

"We are…see you in a few."

Annie turned to Zeke and said, "Well the church lady is with dad, I wonder if she toted a casserole today?"

Zeke turned to her watching her expression, it seemed soft as she said those words.

"So no sarcasm about the church lady today?"

"No sarcasm Zeke. God's really been working on my heart and I want my dad to be happy and if she makes him happy then I can love a church lady too."

And with those last few words, Zeke pulled into the circular driveway that curved in front of the home.

Annie jumped out before Zeke could open her door but she stopped herself and waited for him to catch up. She grabbed his hand and they walked up the front porch steps, Annie noticing that she needed to give them another coat of paint again.

As she was gazing down on the steps she felt Zeke stop and let go of her hand. Turning towards him she saw him frozen in his steps staring at the church lady.

"Mom?" he said.

Judy also looked surprised and returned the same question, "Zeke?"

Stan and Annie looked at each other in amazement. What had just happened here?

Annie stammered, "The church lady is your mom?"

"Who's the church lady?" Judy asked.

"Never mind Mom, but you never told me you were seeing Annie's dad."

"Well…, I didn't want to say anything until I knew it was serious."

Annie panicked when she heard the word serious.

"Pops?" Annie looked at him with an inquiring gaze.

Stan put his arm around Judy and with great joy in his eyes told his daughter and Zeke that they had feelings for each other and wanted to give this relationship time to develop.

Zeke immediately grabbed Annie thinking she would get weak at the knees. But, she stood firm and smiled letting him know that everything was okay.

Later, when they were alone, Annie started to giggle as she and Zeke were talking about their day.

"You do realize Zeke that if they marry, your mom will be my mother-in-law and my stepmom."

Zeke looked over at her and said, "And you also realize that if you marry me you will become one of those casserole toting church ladies."

"Not exactly, she said, I won't be single."

Zeke leaned over and kissed her deeply. "You're right, you won't be single, but for the record, I do like casseroles."

"What we suffer now is nothing compared
to the glory He will reveal to us later." Romans 8:18

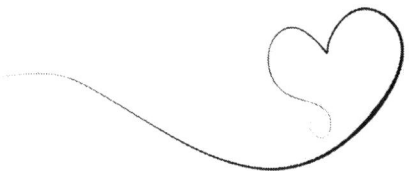

Pink Lipstick in a Pine Box...

The clothes line was in full view outside her bedroom window. Both daughters' clothes had been washed and hung out to dry in the summer breeze. Junie McClain was almost envious of the dresses moving freely outside while she lay dying. Now, no one even the doctor told her for sure she was dying... but she knew. Deep down in her gut she figured since the rheumatic fever stole most of her childhood and then asthma took its hold, her days were numbered a good bit shorter than some. She made up her mind that she didn't want to be bitter over dying young; she only wanted to know the sweetness of greeting her Maker.

Junie also wanted to write her final wishes... for there were some things that she wanted done and some things that needed saying, but she was just so dreadfully weak. With determination that came only from God himself she picked up pencil and paper and with an unsteady hand wrote out her request.

"Holice... these are my plans I want you to carry out as near as you can. First, I want my sister, Effie to take the children. Holice you work and give Effie the money to feed, dress and school them. Please do all in your power to help her bring them up in the right way and you live before them like a father should. I hope the children will love and help you in every way and when you're too disabled to work, they will give you a home. I hope the children will not give you any trouble and will make good Christian girls... I want you all to meet me in heaven. Please dress me in pink or white for the funeral and please thank everyone who ever helped me during my sickness."

Not very eloquent, but then Junie was plain and simple. She and Holice were sharecroppers who lived more basic than some. Junie wore plain cotton print dresses; her brown hair was cut short and her bangs held back with a bobby pin. Her smile and quick wit was contagious on her petite frame that was almost too big for her size four feet to carry. Her only adornment was her thin gold wedding band that held no shine against her inner glow.

Junie also decided to die plain. No need to change now. Just a pink or white dress would probably be enough to spruce up the simple pine box she'd be lying in. She wanted Effie to put a tad bit of pink lipstick on her because even if a woman is dead she certainly wants to look her best. Junie was like most women in the area of compliments, she liked getting them on occasion and even though she wouldn't be able to hear them... she wanted them said nonetheless.

She laid her head back on the soft cotton pillows. She could tell as she gasped for breath that death was minutes away. She looked over and saw her husband Holice, grief already etched in his eyes... he was holding their three-year old daughter, Shirley in his arms. Six-year old Julia was standing next to her head.

"Mama", Julia said, "do you see angels yet?"

"None yet honey, but I hear their wings... can you hear the swooshing sound Julia?" Junie barely whispered out.

Julia just stood there looking around trying to see angels or hear their wings.

"Holice," Junie whispered, "would you and the girls lie beside me; I want to meet Jesus with my family in my arms."

Holice laid Shirley next to her as Julia also climbed in. He slid next to Junie and held her in his arms.

"Mama," Julia squealed breathlessly, " I hear the angels wings... do you hear them?"

"Yes baby, I do"

In that instant, Junie was gone.

Holice began sobbing and when the girls saw this they began to cry also... too young to truly understand the full impact of their heartbreaking loss.

With great sadness, Effie did as promised and dressed Junie who was barely 37 years old in her best white cotton dress. She dabbed a little pink lipstick on her lips and then put just a little on her colorless cheeks to match. Then Junie McClain was gently placed in her simple pine box on August 23, 1942.

"Oh, Junie," Effie said, "you are the prettiest thing, everyone will say so."

As Effie looked upon her sister, she almost swore Junie smiled ever-so-slightly.

"This is my commandment, that you love
one another as I have loved you." John 15:12

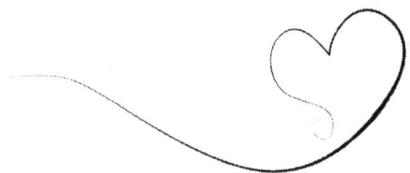

Seeing What God Sees...

"Pour my truth into her Libby. Speak life into her heart," spoke God.

"What Lord?"

"Give her your time."

"Who Lord?"

"Patti."

"Ohhh, Lord…her?"

"Yes."

"But Lord, she's just awful, always bragging, tells outrageous stories, wears the gaudiest clothes for attention and is so obnoxiously loud." I felt myself begging for release.

"I trust you, Libby."

"Ohhh, Lord," Libby moaned as she sucked in her breath and prepared for what?

It didn't take long for the 'what' to appear as Patti Pugh swooped into the church with a bright red top showing a bit of cleavage, accentuated with gold dangly earrings, and had enough bracelets to join the bell choir. Patti's lovely blonde hair was pulled back in a pony-tail that showed her pretty forty-something face. With eyebrows arched and bright red lipstick glossed on, it actually took away from her physical beauty. Couldn't she see that?

"Pour into her Libby," God whispered.

Libby walked over to Patti and sat beside her in the worn wooden pew.

"Do you mind?" she asked.

Patti shook her head no and half smiled.

"Are you having a good morning so far?" Libby asked trying to ease into conversation.

Patti looked sad as she tilted her head down and allowed a tear to drop on her knee.

Libby hesitated thinking, "Should I ask what's wrong or just let her be?"

"Pour into her." God whispered again.

Putting her hand on top of Patti's, Libby asked her what was wrong.

Patti's bottom lip trembled with emotion.

"I met my birth parents this week and they asked that I never visit them again."

"Ohhh, Lord, its deep rejection."

"And," she continued, "My adoptive parents are hurt and angry with me."

"More rejection, Lord." Libby gripped her hand tighter as she spoke.

Patti took a deep breath, then let out a grievous sob, "My husband, John, doesn't understand me at all and has asked for a divorce."

Libby's heart ripped for the hurt Patti carried.

Patti then stopped and looked into her face, "Why do you ask? You've never cared before. You and your friends always make me feel invisible."

Her blunt honesty cut to the core of Libby's soul. Tears welled up in her eyes and she felt so ashamed.

"Patti, please forgive me for being judgmental, I care greatly but more importantly, God cares."

Patti smiled slightly and said, "Please forgive me Libby, for I have also judged you."

"You did? In what way?" Libby responded in a greatly shocked voice.

"Well," Patti said, "I thought you were an up-tight, self-righteous, I'm better-than-you Christian."

Stunned from head to toe, Libby had no idea she was perceived that way, but was Patti speaking the truth? Did others see her that way? Did she carry a pious heart? Her spirit groaned under conviction.

Libby's eyes swam with tears as she asked Patti to forgive her and start over.

Patti smiled and said, "of course," as she pulled out a tissue from her red purse and dabbed her own eyes. They both sat a while longer sharing until Libby stood up and looked at her watch saying, "How about some lunch? I know a great sandwich place to swap stories as we eat." she said grinning.

Patti smiled, "Well, won't we look a bit odd since you're way more conservative looking and I'm rather bold and flashy?"

Libby grabbed her arm as they walked out the church doors saying, "I'm thinking that's a great recipe for a new friendship!"

Later that night Libby thought, "Whew Lord, that was tough, so who exactly was to pour into whom?"

God replied. "I asked you to pour truth into Patti."

"I asked Patti to pour truth into you."

"Therefore, if anyone is in Christ, he is a new creation; the old has gone, the new has come!" 1 Corinthians 5:17

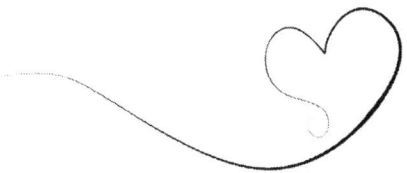

What could be Better than Sweet Tea?

Everyone called her 'Sugah' Queen. Sugah being all the white, granulated deliciousness she used as she canned everything from figs to vegetables. As you well know, in the South everything is sweeter. Queen was her last name, Maybelle Edith Queen to be exact, but from the time she was old enough to cook, the name Sugah stuck and no one ever heard her first name again. That was okay with her, except she did love her middle name, 'Edith.' Actually it wasn't her given name, she just loved the name Edith and added it when she signed her name on papers. Her second daughter, Barbara, actually named her middle child, Mary Edith. Sugah just chuckled to herself as she never did tell her it wasn't her birth name. Oh, how she was proud to have a grandchild named after her.

Sugah, now in her mid-nineties sat in her well-worn rocking chair on the front porch. She loved her porch, where she could sit and wave to the neighbors, ponder on their day, and ask the Good Lord to bless them. Sugah would always have her glass of sweet tea and not worry about the extra sugar she put in her glass. She was ninety-five after all who cared if she had extra?

On this particular day, September 05, 2015, she was just plum worn out from all the fried pies she'd cooked for the sick people in the church. They loved her fried pies and she didn't want to disappoint them, so she fried until her arthritic hands could do no more. She laid them on paper towels to soak up the extra grease, made her glass of sweet tea and headed to the porch. She needed to rest awhile so she pushed her rocker behind the oak tree so the neighbors wouldn't see her doing 'nuthin,' what would they think of her? She never wanted anyone to think she was lazy!

Sugah eased herself down onto her rocker, loving the new cushions her daughters had bought for it. The thickness of the cushions felt good on her bones. She had gotten so thin over the past few years, she didn't have enough fat to cushion her backside. The Good Lord knew she was appreciative. Sugah leaned her head back after taking a swig of her sweet tea nectar and just 'rested' her eyes a bit. The air had a coolness to it which felt good blowing across her face. "Just for a minute," she thought as she shut her tired eyes and thought about her life.

***

"Sugah?" he inquired. "Is that you?"

Leaning over the watermelons at the roadside fruit stand, Sugah stood up quickly and brushed her coal black hair out of her eyes. Her dress was simple but clean, made from a blue calico cotton her mother had purchased. Sugah was a pretty young woman, not beautiful like her friend Ester, but pretty enough to catch the eye of a man for sure.

Sugah eyed the young man trying to figure out if she knew him.

"Yes, that's me," she said with a skeptical look on her face.

Floyd leaned back on one leg and crossed his arms. He knew he was instantly smitten with this girl, but he was a bit older and didn't want to scare her away. So he smiled real big and said, "I thought I recognized a Queen girl. I'm Floyd Tanner, my dad Bobby worked with your dad at the old mill in town a few years ago.

Sugah smiled as she recalled her dad's relationship with his dad. "Oh yes, I remember your dad, but I don't remember meeting you."

"Oh you did Sugah, but you were only about eight, and I was eighteen." He waited for a response, hoping it would be a good one.

Sugah eyed Floyd with thoughts flying through her head. Handsome in a cocky, self-assured kind of way. Medium frame with reddish brown hair with a few freckles splattered on his face. Had to be about twenty-eight and apparently not married according to his left hand. Wonder what's wrong with him?

Floyd saw the puzzled look on her face and wondered what she was thinking.

With a smile only Sugah could flash, she stuck out her hand and said, "Well, it's nice to meet ya, Floyd Tanner."

And that was all it took, a look, a smile, and love bloomed instantly. One year later they were married, for better or worse, they were husband and wife. It was after the, "I do," that the worst brewed and boy, did it brew.

Floyd was a good man. He had a good name in the community and was well respected. However, his mother was a difficult woman to say the least, a widow with a need to be number one at all times. But, with Sugah now in her son's life, she was pushed to number two and didn't like it one bit. No siree, not one bit.

While the courtship was going on, Floyd knew Sugah was the one for him, so he built a home on the family property. Not a big home, mind you, but one that Sugah loved. Sugah was a doer and Floyd built her a store to run, just a small general type store that she adored. She made a nice amount to help out with the family expenses, but from time to time, her money would come up missing. At first, it was small amounts making Sugah think it was a mistake in her figuring. But, after a while, it became clear is was not her figuring it was someone stealing.

But who would steal from her and Floyd? Sadly, she had her suspicions.

The next Saturday when Sugah did her weekly total, her balance was $130 profit. She took out $13 for her church tithe, tied up the rest in a burlap bag and hid it under her bed. She only told Floyd but made sure his mother was within ear shot.

Sunday morning Sugah reached under her bed and grabbed the burlap bag. She counted her money knowing less her tithe she should have $117 remaining. She did not...a twenty was gone. Her heart sank for she knew Eunice took the money. She knew Eunice didn't care for her as it was evident in what she told others behind her back, but to steal from her? Heartbreaking.

When she told Floyd, he didn't believe her. He said her figuring was off. Sugah was devastated that he didn't back her up.

How could she manage to deal with Eunice and forgive her? And how would she ever convince Floyd and forgive him for not backing her? Thank goodness it was Sunday, she needed a good sermon to soothe her soul.

Sugah slid into the back pew at exactly 11:00a.m., not wanting to speak to her friends at the moment. She was exhausted, not from her constant physical work, but emotionally she was drained to the core.

"Lord help me," was all she could muster in prayer.

Tears ran down her young cheeks. "Why did life have to be so hard at times?" Sugah shifted in her seat and sadness seemed to saturate her body as she pondered over her relationship with Eunice. God knew how much she wanted a sweet union between them. They both loved Floyd, so why couldn't they love each other? The strain was just too much and her heart too heavy to stay. She picked up her purse and left walking the half mile home.

On her way, God prompted her to go to Eunice and talk with her.

Sugah walked up the long rocky driveway and knocked on her door. Eunice opened with a grimace on her face. "What do you want?"

"Eunice, could we talk out here on the porch?"

Eunice reluctantly nodded her head and sat on one of her porch rockers. Sugah stood figuring she could make a dash if Eunice became angry.

"Eunice, why don't you like me? I so want us to at least like each other."

Eunice just sat and stared.

"Please say something Eunice." Sugah pleaded.

Eunice looked up and with tears in her eyes said, "You took my son away, I have no one to take care of me since his daddy died." "You have him all the time and I have nothing."

Sugah's heart sank as she thought, "God please give me the right words."

"Eunice, you haven't lost him, he will always be your son, and maybe you could consider me a daughter?"

"Did you take the money to make me look bad Eunice?"

She nodded yes.

"Well, it worked Eunice, Floyd didn't believe you would do that."
"He took your side and not mine."

Eunice thought she would feel happy to hear those words, but it made her feel worse.

"I'm sorry Sugah, can you ever forgive me?"

Sugah bent down and put her hands on top of hers and said, "Of course, and the money issue will be our secret."

Eunice smiled as she went back in to fix Sugah a glass of sweet tea. It was the beginning of a new relationship that lasted until the day Eunice died. Even on her deathbed, she took her daughter-in-law's hand and said, "I loved you like a daughter."

***

Sugah opened her eyes from 'resting them a bit,' realizing had it not been for Eunice she may never have learned so many tough life lessons. The main one being forgiveness. She had to learn to forgive many a soul, but none were tougher than Eunice. But, the harder the lesson, the sweeter the reward…and Sugah knew all about the sweet.

"Favour is deceitful, and beauty is vain: but a woman that feareth the Lord, she shall be praised." Proverbs 31:30

Meet the Author

Inspiration has always been Lisa's heart. Inspiring people through words of faith and love is her passion. Lisa has been writing for the Georgia Mountain Laurel magazine for a few years and is grateful for this tremendous blessing.

She and her husband Tony love to visit Bed & Breakfast Inns for weekend adventures, hunt for primitive treasures, entertain friends and enjoy their grown son Joel and soon-to-be driving son, Luke. Lisa would love to hear from you. You can reach her by sending an e-mail to bless_your_heart@yahoo.com

24523452R10104

Made in the USA
San Bernardino, CA
28 September 2015